COUGAR MOM

A Romantic Suspense Novel

EVE LANGLAIS

Copyright © 2018/19, Eve Langlais

Cover Art Razz Dazz Design © 2018

Produced in Canada

Published by Eve Langlais ~ www.EveLanglais.com

eBook ISBN: 978 177 384 129 8

Print ISBN: 978 177 384 130 4

AUTHOR'S NOTE

If you've been following the ladies of Killer Moms, you know they haven't lived simple, peaceful lives. Each of them has a past they escaped and adversity they've had to overcome. Each of these moms was recruited by the KM agency for a reason with an end goal that always centered around their children.

Meredith's past is a little darker than some of the others, and it might be difficult for those who've experienced abusive situation. How she overcomes it makes her happily ever after that much sweeter.

Some of her recollections may be difficult for some readers to read, but I hope you will join Meredith on her journey and celebrate the happily ever after she deserves.

Without further ado...I give you, Cougar Mom.

PROLOGUE

TWENTY-THREE YEARS AGO, when everything *went to hell.*

The jail cell smelled of piss and despair and proved noisier than expected. Despite having a concrete box to herself, the open bars in the window meant that Anita got to hear everything happening outside her door. Lots of crying, some screaming, even laughter—which, in a place like this, seemed impossible.

This wasn't somewhere to entertain hope.

The hard bed boasted only the thinnest mattress and barely cushioned her butt as she hugged her legs to her chest. She didn't have a roommate.

Yet.

But she'd been warned to expect one. Told to forget the very concept of privacy. The toilet in the corner had no stall, nothing to hide her.

She'd screwed up, and now she would pay the

price. Better get used to it. Twenty to life was the worst-case scenario. Her lawyer said that if she pled guilty, she might get less. Eight to ten, with a chance for early parole for good behavior. But would a judge agree to a lighter sentence?

The case against Anita was open and shut. Anita had called the police herself—*"Hello, I think I killed my boyfriend."* When the cops arrived, she didn't argue or protest in any way. She handed over the baby before she held out her hands to be cuffed, still wearing Tommy's blood, making no apologies for what she'd done.

When the detective questioning her asked why she killed her boyfriend, at only twenty-two years old and already the mother of two, she said, "Because he deserved it."

There must be something wrong with her because she didn't feel guilty about what she'd done. Actually, there was a certain satisfaction in knowing that the abusive jerk was dead. It kind of made her wish that she'd acted earlier. And not just with Tommy. So many awful things in her life could have been prevented if she'd pulled a knife and said, *"enough."*

Her lawyer argued it was self-defense. Problem was, she didn't have any bruises on her. Her lawyer claimed she suffered from battered spouse syndrome. The defense lawyer cited that she had no emergency room record or police reports that alleged abuse.

How arrogant of that bitch in her suit to think

Anita had the freedom to call for help. The woman who claimed Anita lied about the abusive behavior had obviously never been willing to do anything to avoid being punched so hard she blacked out. Clearly, never had someone imprison them if they bruised. Anita wasn't allowed to leave the apartment until it healed.

There wasn't much questioning of the kids. The baby was only eighteen months old and not exactly a good witness. As for Donovan, five years old and very serious for his age, he wouldn't speak to the social workers. Wouldn't tell them if Mommy or Daddy left the marks on his body.

But Tommy's mother had no problem opening her yap.

She painted a picture of a sweet man who did his best by his family, despite his whoring bitch of a girlfriend who was an unfit parent.

The person who'd changed every diaper, burped after every feeding, and stayed up countless nights walking her babies was the unfit one?

Tommy's mother, Agnes, took the credit for the children's upbringing, claimed she was the one to care for them while Anita partied and did drugs.

"She's lying." Anita still didn't regret the outburst in court, even as the judge rebuked her. When her lawyer jumped in, they offered to have Anita pee in a cup to prove the claims false. The prosecution argued that she'd been in custody too long for the drugs to still appear.

3

The truth couldn't be proven. Even in death, Tommy kept beating her.

The day of her sentencing, Anita waited in the cell, dressed in the coarse orange jumpsuit that clashed with her bright auburn hair. Her eyes were red-rimmed from the lawyer's news that Tommy's mom had won custody of the kids, and the judgement wasn't even dependent on the outcome of Anita's trial.

Her babies in the hands of that awful woman... She'd seen them once since her arrest when her lawyer managed to have child protective services bring them for a visit. The baby had no idea and babbled happily on her lap; her sweet little Carolina unaware of what had happened. But at five, Donovan understood too much.

The kid who wouldn't talk to anyone lisped, "It's my fault."

Anita could hear in his voice that he genuinely believed that. He thought he was the reason his mommy sat in jail.

She started to cry, which led to the guards coming over and trying to take away her kids. Whereupon, she snapped. Made an unfortunate scene that got her banned from seeing them again.

Some days, Anita wondered why she didn't do like the girl in the next cell block over had done: hang herself with a sheet from her bunk. What was the point? The judge on the case hated her. Anita was about to get slapped with the maximum sentence and would never see her babies again.

Her knees pressed hard into her eye sockets as she sought a way to shrink into nothing.

She heard the heels long before she saw the person wearing them. Clack. Clack. The female lawyers liked to wear the fancy shoes that gave them a few inches. Strutted in their tailored business suits that screamed, *"look at me compared to you."*

Anita wanted to be like those women. Strong. Powerful. Unafraid. Instead, she was done before she had a chance to get started.

The shoes stopped near her cell, and there was some clanking as the door slid open. Super worrisome. She wasn't supposed to go to court for a few hours yet.

She lifted her head to peek at the person in the doorway. A woman, a few years older than Anita. She had the smoothest brown skin and almond-shaped eyes Anita had ever seen. Her hair was tucked up in a complicated chignon that allowed some escaping curls, and her outfit was stylish if bold, the mango color bright in the bland space.

She looked like a fancy lawyer. And for some reason, she'd stopped by Anita's cell.

"Can I help you?"

"Are you Anita Whittaker?"

"Yeah." Seemed kind of stupid to deny it.

"You killed your boyfriend."

Anita's gaze narrowed. "Who are you? Why are

5

you in my cell?" Because this was odd. The woman was inside with her, not across a table with Anita shackled. Nor did she have a guard, his hand resting on the butt of his weapon, standing anywhere close.

"What would you say if I told you I could get you out of this cell and reunite you with your children?"

"I'd say you're being cruel." How dare this woman taunt her with the impossible. Anita would give anything to be with her babies again.

"I assure you, it's possible. But for it to happen, you have to trust me."

Trust this smart-looking woman in a suit? Had to be a lawyer—and pricey she'd bet, too. "I don't have the kind of money it would take to pay you."

"It won't cost you a penny."

The snort emerged from Anita with no control. "Nothing is ever free."

"Would you feel better if I said the people I work for, the ones who can help, will take payment via work."

"Work?" Anita arched a brow. "I should warn you that, according to my ex-boyfriend, I suck at sex." Because she knew the type of work they likely wanted her to do. She had no skills. No real value other than her looks. And even those had taken a beating.

The woman's full lips curved. "Your ex, Tommy, was an asshole."

Anita blinked.

The woman went on. "He deserved what you did

to him and more. Which is the only reason we're offering this deal. Do you want to accept it or not?"

In a few hours, a judge would send Anita to jail. She'd never see her babies again. Or she could jump off a cliff and trust this woman to do as she said.

"Get me out of here. I'll do anything to get back with my kids."

"Glad to hear it." The woman opened the handbag by her side and pulled out a bundle of clothes. "Change, and we'll leave."

"Now?" It couldn't be that quick. There was paperwork to do, probably some more time in front of a judge.

"Yes, now. No point in wasting more time."

Anita eyed the woman. "Mind turning around, then?"

Those lips curved again. "You'll have to lose that shyness if you're going to work out." The woman turned, and Anita quickly shimmied out of the jump-suit and into a pair of soft track pants, a sports bra, and a comfortable sweater. The light shoes were nice, as were the clean underwear and socks.

She could almost believe when she was done dressing that this woman could actually do as she said. "I'm ready."

The woman gave her a glance. "Follow me." She stepped from the cell.

Anita hesitated. She still didn't see a guard.

It was rather early.

Anita took cautious steps out of the cell. The woman waited a few paces away. The hall was the quietest Anita had ever heard it.

"Let's go. The plane won't wait forever."

"Plane?" Anita's feet stumbled to follow.

"We're going on a private charter."

"To where? You promised I'd be with my babies."

"Your kids will join you shortly. They need to take a commercial flight and then disappear on the ground."

"You make it sound like some top-secret operation," she said with a nervous giggle as they neared the door at the end of the hall. She still hadn't seen a single guard.

The door buzzed and opened as they reached it.

The woman stepped through, then paused as she realized that Anita didn't follow.

Cold feet kept her from blindly going any farther. "Who are you?" Anita asked.

"You may call me Marie."

"And where are we going?"

"To see Mother, of course."

"Mother?" Only as they made it out of the prison complex did Anita clue into what it meant.

"So, this *is* a sex thing, after all."

"The agency would never ask one of its moms to do something like that. Although, I can tell you from personal experience that it's easier to eliminate a target in bed when they're not expecting it." Marie winked.

"You do realize you just implied that you murder people?"

"If contracted. And you will be able to eliminate anyone we ask by the time we're done training you." Marie stopped by a long, black sedan with tinted windows. The interior looked absolutely lavish.

"I can't be an assassin." Anita shook her head. "I'll get arrested again."

Marie snorted. "Only if you do it wrong. And hit jobs aren't the only thing we're called on to do."

"You said something about an agency."

"Killer Moms. Run and operated by mothers, like you and I, down on our luck and in need of a second chance."

"How is murdering people a second chance?"

A mischievous smile lit Marie's lips. "Don't knock it until you try it."

"So, you're one of their agents?"

"If you want to know more, you'll have to get in the car and come with me."

"If I don't?"

"Then walk away."

"And go where? Do what?" She eyed the lavish car. Pondered the insane offer. Thought of how she'd felt while killing Tommy. Nothing. There was only one thing left to say. "What does it pay?"

CHAPTER ONE

T-MINUS SEVEN DAYS until the wedding.

THE BINDER WITH THE NOTES AND DETAILS bounced on the bed where she flung it. The flowered coverlet was a clash of greens and pinks. It matched the art unevenly balanced on the whitewashed walls. It took the tropical theme to the max. But that was what people expected in a resort.

Tired after a long day of heat and preparation, Meredith kicked off her shoes and headed for the balcony. She'd requested and gotten an ocean-view. The salty tang of the air filled her senses and she got to see the sun setting against the horizon. Utterly beautiful.

She should take a moment to enjoy the beach. She deserved it after a day spent making sure everything would run perfectly for Carla's upcoming destination wedding. An evening swim would be just the thing, the warm water soothing to her tired body. Forty-five might be great, but she didn't have the stamina she did in her twenties.

One thing that never changed was how she didn't dare go for a dip when the sun rode high in the sky. A natural redhead, she burned a lovely shade of lobster. At night was when she got to do the things others did in the Caribbean. Like swimming in the ocean.

She hurried for the set of drawers and changed out of her light linen dress and panties to slip on the designer swimsuit. She'd finally given up on bikinis given the scar she couldn't quite hide across her ribs. Who knew a teenage daughter would be so jealous that her widowed father would take up with a stranger instead of his own flesh and blood?

They both got what they deserved.

Meredith grabbed a towel and quickly left her room, skipping down the stairs. The resort was well placed, sitting right on the beach. Meredith arranged for their party to get all the best rooms. Tanya helped hack the computer to make the arrangements.

Everyone pitched in, especially since no one ever expected Carla to get married and retire from Killer Moms. Super shocking. And her choice of getting hitched on a beach took coordinating.

As part of her gift, Meredith had offered to help. She had lots of experience organizing events—and missions. That experience dictated that hands-on was best, hence why she was here before everyone else, talking to the staff, double-checking the details, scouting spots where a sniper could take out a target.

Because this Cougar Mom had a job to do in paradise. Mother, her handler, had acquired a mission that coincided with the dates for the nuptials. She'd transferred Meredith the file only the day before her departure and then insisted on a briefing.

"You'll be using the wedding as your cover," Mother stated as soon as they managed a secure connection.

"And a hello to you, too."

"We spoke in person, not even an hour ago," Marie Cadeaux stated with an exaggerated sigh.

Meredith grinned. *"And? Manners are for friends, too."*

"I am not calling as a friend but as your boss. We have a mission."

"What're the details?" Meredith asked as she finished tying the quail that she'd stuffed with sausage, rice, and herbs. It would be delicious served with some veggies. A fancy feast for one person.

The screen that projected from her marble countertop changed views. It was an expensive little extra when she had the kitchen custom-designed, but it made accessing her recipes so easy—and it could do video chats in a pinch.

A picture appeared of a man, his hair close-cropped,

a light brown, maybe blond in the right light. He wore a suit, layered with an overcoat as he exited an expensive sedan.

"Is that the muscle?" Meredith asked, noting the thickness of him.

"That's the target, the elusive Mr. Laurentian."

"Not so elusive if you got a picture."

"A rare one. Cameras have a tendency to misbehave in his vicinity."

"That's interesting," Meredith claimed as she washed her hands.

"There are a lot of interesting things about Mr. Laurentian," Marie declared. Years later, and they still worked together, Meredith choosing to remain active in the field unlike Marie, who went into management.

"Who is he? What has he done?"

"No one's quite sure. You might say he's a bit of an enigma. He came out of nowhere about fifteen years ago. He is currently based out of New York, with offices around the world, but it appears the island you're about to visit is his main base of operation. He has dual citizenship, which is odd, given he appears to be of French origin."

"What does he dabble in?" Meredith asked, leaning closer to swipe the screen and take notice of the finer details. The strong line of his jaw. The slight tilt to his nose as if he'd broken it before. The way he towered over people when he stood beside them.

"On paper, it looks like he's really good at buying

14

and selling stocks, plus acquiring properties at rock-bottom prices."

"Then reselling them high?"

"Not exactly. He turns them into viable businesses or low-rent apartment buildings that are heavily subsidized."

"Sounds like he's a good guy."

"In most respects, he is. Except we haven't been able to discern where his initial investments came from. Just like we can't figure out how, with all the money he basically donates, the man remains filthy rich. The assumption is he has another business that funds his activities."

"Dirty money." It existed everywhere there was a market for vice.

"Maybe. And not the main focus of our task. There is a contract to terminate."

Someone wanted Mr. Laurentian dead.

The recollection faded to the background as Meredith hit the beach. This time of night, only a few people were on it, including someone with the rolled-up pants of a tourist, who was exchanging something with a rather scruffy fellow.

Probably a drug deal.

She marked their location and appearance for reporting later. The last thing they needed was some kind of drug war during the wedding.

The fellow with the rolled pants headed back to the resort and cast her only a quick glance before continuing on his way.

The sun was setting, bathing everything in an orange glow. She dropped her towel on the sand and kicked off her sandals. She'd not brought a weapon, not with her building in sight and the inability to hide it.

The undulating waves beckoned, the tug of them gentle and sucking at the sand under her toes.

She waded into the warm surf and, as soon as she could, began to float, stroking through the water. The twilight eased into full dark, meaning she wasn't exactly visible, especially given how far out she'd swum from shore, which meant that when the Sea-Doo came out of nowhere, she assumed it didn't see her.

She managed to avoid it and, treading water, yelled, "Hey, watch where you're going!" Marine rules stated that vessels on the water after dark must have lights.

As if hearing her, the watercraft flipped around and came barreling again for her.

Meredith knew better than to panic. She began swimming for shore, which proved increasingly difficult with the agitation of the water as the Sea-Doo circled her. The jerk was doing donuts, and the waves tossed her around.

Rather than fight them, Meredith dove underwater and swam, but she couldn't hold her breath forever. She surfaced, and as if the person on the watercraft waited for her, it came screaming towards Meredith. This time, she couldn't avoid it, and it clipped her hard enough that she saw darkness.

She blinked her eyes and noticed filmy white curtains all around. Mosquito netting and a bed. Both unfamiliar.

Where am I?

A face leaned over her, tanned and handsome. Short-cropped hair. Blond. A square jaw and a nose slightly hitched as if once broken. The man seemed familiar. Concern filled his gaze. "You're awake. How do you feel?" his deep voice purred.

It did things to her. Made her feel horny. Maybe not the best thing to admit aloud. Not to a stranger at any rate. Or was he someone she knew?

"Who are you?" she asked. Only to frown. Her mind struggled to answer an even more fundamental question. "Who am I?"

There was something utterly frightening in that moment as she struggled to recall even something as basic as her name. She hyperventilated. "Who am I?" she cried again at the man. Surely, he would know.

"You tell me."

She would have, except... "I don't remember."

CHAPTER TWO

HUGO WANTED to curse as the woman obviously played him for a fool. To think he'd felt sorry for her when he found her washed up on the beach. And now, she pretended to have forgotten her name. Such an obvious ploy.

"Nice try, lady. I don't know who you are," he said, straightening. "I found you passed out on the beach about to be dragged out into the ocean. Not the safest thing. You could have drowned."

"Then I guess I should thank you for saving me." Her brow creased. "What happened?"

"You tell me. Were you drinking?" It happened all the time. Tourists came here and seemed to forget their limits, and the resorts didn't help with their unlimited alcoholic offerings.

"I don't know. Do I smell like booze?"

"I am not sniffing your breath." He leaned away

and crossed his arms. When he carried her earlier, he'd not noticed any lingering scent of liquor, but not all of them left a stench.

"My head hurts like I'm hungover," she moaned.

"Booze or drugs, doesn't really matter. You should learn to control your vices."

"Do you think that's why I can't remember anything?" Her eyes widened in feigned fear. She did a great job of acting. "Maybe I got a dose of something bad."

Or maybe she was full of shit. "I've already called emergency services. They should be on their way eventually."

"What do you mean...eventually?" she asked as she sat up and put a hand to her head, overdoing the act in his opinion.

"Meaning there is only one working ambulance currently, and it had to transport someone clear across the island to the airport for an emergency departure."

"I don't need an ambulance," she grumbled, still palpating her head. "I have a headache, probably because of the lump."

"What lump?"

"As if you didn't notice. It's huge. Did you hit me?" The suspicion in her eyes almost looked real.

He snorted. "Nice try. Who did it? You, or your accomplice? Are they about to rush in and make accusations?"

It took her a moment to grasp his implication. "I

did not hit myself." Then an even bigger lightbulb widened her gaze. "You think I'm lying."

"I am not a fucking idiot," he said with a sarcastic drawl. "Amnesia is nineties soap opera shit. It doesn't happen in real life."

"What would you know about soap operas?" she inquired.

"I used to be a big wrestling fan back in the day. And even they did the amnesia thing. It's a cheap gimmick, and an obvious one. Meaning, I am not falling for it. So, you can take yourself and your fabrications and wait for the ambulance on the porch, or leave since your plot failed. I will mention, this house is fully equipped with cameras, meaning you can't accuse me of anything later in order to extort money from me."

"I would never," she huffed. "What kind of pathetic life do you have that you think everyone is out to cheat you?" Rising from the bed, he had time to note her lithe body in the swimsuit. He'd not dared change her and had just tossed a blanket over her shivering frame.

With her awake, though, he could finally take full note. Beautiful woman, tall, slim. Not young, perhaps her late thirties, early forties. Her wet hair hung down her back, dark in the dim light. Her bathing suit molded to her firm body. He handed her the robe he kept nearby.

"That's priceless, the woman faking amnesia calling me pathetic. I've encountered your kind before, pretending and acting to extort money. Unfortunately for you, I learned from each experience."

"I would never blackmail."

"How would you know if you can't remember?" he taunted. "Now, get moving before I call the cops."

She glared as she snatched the robe and tried to slot her arms into the sleeves. It took her a few tries where her eyes crossed, and she swayed. Then she simply stood there, looking forlorn in the oversized garment. "I think I should sit down."

"You can sit outside." He didn't fall for the act.

She took a step to the door, her gaze a little vacant. She swayed.

Despite his misgivings, he steadied her lest she slam into the small table with the expensive vase.

She felt clammy to the touch. He could see her temple and the blood trickling from it. That wasn't fake.

Still, he released her and stepped back. Some people would go to any lengths.

She exited the room and paused. "Where do I go?"

"You can sit on the porch and wait for the ambulance or call yourself a ride."

"But where will I go? I have no money. No identification. I don't know where I live." With each statement, her voice hitched.

His resolve hardened. "Stop the act."

Her shoulder slumped. "I wish it were an act. I really can't remember."

With him following, she exited the guest bedroom, head tucked, not once looking around at the décor. If he didn't know better, he'd say she watched her feet.

The front door loomed, and her shoulders slumped at the sight of it. But she didn't argue as he held it open and ushered her out. It slammed shut, but that wasn't enough. He locked it, too.

What was she doing? He could have gone to his office and watched via one of the many cameras. But, instead, he stood watching her from behind the curtains in the living room for some reason. She eschewed the facing chairs with the little table between them to sit on the step, a huddled figure in plush terrycloth. She hugged her knees.

Still acting. She stayed there, barely moving during the forty minutes it took for the ambulance to arrive. She took the charade the whole way.

The next day, the police showed up. His butler knocked on his office door to inform him.

"Sir, Superintendent Pierrot is here to speak with you."

"About what?" he snapped. "I'm a busy man." And Pierrot liked to talk, then hint about how his department could really use some new piece of equipment or another until Hugo agreed to buy it for the man. Why he didn't just send him an email request, Hugo would never understand.

"He has questions about the woman picked up on the property last night."

"Oh, for fuck's sake. She better not have accused me of anything." Hugo rubbed the spot between his brows, feeling a headache forming. He'd not gotten enough sleep. He never did these days. A restlessness had invaded his spirit and dreams, making it impossible for him to get more than a few hours at a time.

"What should I tell him?"

Tempting as it was to tell Pierrot to fuck off, Hugo sighed. "Send him in."

It took less than a minute for the high-ranking policeman to enter his office. Hugo eyed Pierrot, a dark-skinned man who remained fit despite the pressure of his position. As a male in his late forties, Hugo knew how hard that could be. "Superintendent, to what do I owe the honor of this visit?"

"I am here on official police business. I just left the hospital after speaking to a woman who claims she was on your property last night."

"More like this morning."

"So, you admit to having met her?"

"If we're talking about a tall redhead, then yes, I did. And I don't care what she's accusing me of, I have video footage that shows I never touched her."

Pierrot's brows rose. "No accusation. We're just trying to find out more information. She's lost her memory."

"Has she now?" he said sarcastically. Pierrot shouldn't have been the gullible type.

"She has quite the gash on her head. The doctor

says it's impeding her ability to remember. Since she appeared to have been in the water when her accident occurred, she lacked any form of identification."

"How convenient."

Pierrot's gaze sharpened. "I see you're skeptical, but I think she's telling the truth. She doesn't recall who she is."

"If that's the case, then someone will report her missing." Especially if she turned out to be a tourist, which seemed likely given her pallor. The media would make a big deal about the poor tourist attacked or almost drowned. Never mind that their home countries were no better, they liked to hammer the paradise spots.

"If she travelled here alone, it might be a few days before anyone notices." Hotel staff didn't always keep track of their guests.

"Well, I can't help you. I just found her."

"Where?" Pierrot had taken out a pad and a pen.

"On the beach. Close to where the property line ends."

"What time?"

"Around three a.m."

The pen stopped moving, and the cop's gaze fixed on him. "Why were you on the beach at three a.m., Mr. Laurentian?"

"I couldn't sleep." He only got a few hours a night now. Not that it affected his performance. He was as sharp and fit as ever, just not sleeping. "When

I get restless like that, I like to go for a jog on the beach."

"And you just happened upon a woman washed ashore."

"I don't know if she washed up. I saw her on the sand, the water trying to suck her in. So, I did what anyone would do and carried her to safety." Something he was beginning to regret.

"Was she awake?"

"No."

"Was she already injured?"

It suddenly occurred to him that this was an interrogation. "I did not harm that woman."

"Which you can prove, I assume."

"Shouldn't my word be enough?"

Pierrot shrugged. "It would help if we had, perhaps, some video footage of her discovery to corroborate your version of the events. It would forestall any suspicions that might arise."

His lips flattened. "No cameras, given it was past the edge of my property."

"Meaning, we only have your word that you weren't the one to hit her."

"Why would I hit her?"

"Perhaps you met this woman and partied a little too hard. Could be it was an accident, or things got a little out of hand."

"I don't pick up strangers to bring home. Ever."

"Yet you brought this woman?" Pierrot pounced.

"Because she was unconscious. What else was I supposed to do?" Hugo snapped. "Leave her on the beach?"

"Why not call for help where you found her?"

"For one, I didn't have a phone. And, secondly, she was cold and wet."

"I thought you said she wasn't awake. How would you know she was cold?"

"Because I have fucking eyes." He could still picture how she shivered on the sand.

"How did you transport her here?" Pierrot kept scribbling.

"As I said, I carried her."

"You did?" A disparaging glance in Hugo's direction. "Are you sure you didn't have help? Someone who witnessed what happened?"

"No help," Hugo growled. "Now, if we're done, I have work to do."

"Just one more question."

"What?"

"The policeman's summer barbecue is slated for next month and—"

Hugo cut him off. "Laurentian Enterprises would be delighted to make a donation to our very important local police force. Happy now?"

The police superintendent saw himself out, and Hugo leaned back in his chair with a sigh.

He couldn't believe the captain had actually implied that he'd hurt the woman. He also thought she told the truth. Could Hugo have been wrong about her?

He rang his secretary. Francis answered. "What is it, boss?" No mockery in the tone. Francis would never dare.

"The woman that was here last night. I mean, this morning. Can you find out if she's still at the hospital?" Francis didn't ask what woman. First thing Hugo had done, was advise his staff of the intruder to see if anyone had heard or seen anything.

"Let me have a peek, sir."

Francis didn't bother to put him on hold, simply tapped away on a keyboard before announcing, "She is still a patient. According to her file, she is suffering from cranial trauma with a hematoma on her brain, causing swelling and loss of some cognition."

"I don't suppose you have access to any visitor logs?"

Francis snorted. "You're joking, right?"

He sighed. Things were more relaxed in the tropics. Too relaxed for someone organized like him. "Who's paying for her care?"

"No one. She is being watched after by the state." They wouldn't take a chance on her care in case she was a tourist. They didn't need another negative media piece impacting their tourism.

His conscience niggled at him. He should do something. "Francis, one last thing."

"What is it, boss?"

"Send a fruit basket."

"At once, sir."

"Anonymously."

"Always."

He hung up and drummed his fingers.

The woman wasn't his problem. The business venture he was looking into, though, might prove lucrative.

And he'd just replenished the coffers.

He rang for his lawyer. "Where are we on the legalities for the deal?"

"They've suddenly decided to change the terms and ask for more."

"We're already paying them too much," he said softly.

"Which is the point I made. But they're being insistent, so I was drafting a new agreement with the new sum when you called."

"He's being a pain in my ass," Hugo remarked. "I'll be glad when this is over."

"Only a few more days for the deals to be done."

And then he'd really get to work.

CHAPTER THREE

THE PROBLEM of *who* she was plagued her. Something so simple as her name shouldn't cause her such pain and panic. The blank in her mind acted like a black hole that sucked away any answer before she could glimpse it.

What's my name? That, most of all, eluded her. She wanted to rush away from this hospital bed and scream at people until someone gave her an answer. Surely, she'd be recognized. Missed...

What if she wasn't? What if she was the kind of person everyone hated? She'd seen herself in the mirror, her skin a fine porcelain with not a freckle to be seen. Her hair cut in layers that, after the shower in the hospital, curled slightly in the humidity. The bathing suit she'd been wearing appeared expensive and was her only clue.

A woman of means, which meant that her disappearance wouldn't go unnoticed.

As expected, the police got involved, asking her questions to which she had no answers. They even went so far as to fingerprint her.

Could she be a criminal? She had no way of knowing.

She spent the first day in the hospital being tested, questioned, and resting. The pain medication for the throbbing in her head had a somnolent effect. She drifted in and out, being woken by nurses every so often to ensure she'd not slipped into a coma.

On day two, the policeman returned. It was nice to remember a face and a name for someone.

"Mr. Pierrot." She managed a smile for him from where she sat in a chair by the window overlooking a city both bright and dingy. The air conditioner above the window rattled as it tried to stay ahead of the moist heat. It didn't do a very good job.

"Mademoiselle." There was a burr to the French word. "Please, call me Jacques. We don't believe in being so formal here in the islands. You are looking much better today."

"I feel better." The throbbing headache receding into the background meant that she could take regular acetaminophen instead of the stronger stuff that made her fuzzy.

"Does that mean you've recovered your memories?" he asked, seeming genuinely interested.

She shook her head. "Not yet." It frustrated because not only did she lack an identity, but she also remained ignorant of her capabilities. She didn't even realize that she understood French until a nurse entered her room that morning and began babbling to her in it.

"According to the doctor, these things can take time."

"I know," she said on a sigh. She'd heard the spiel. "He is hopeful once the swelling goes down, I might remember more."

"We've sent off your details, including the prints, to American authorities. European, too."

"Wouldn't my prints being on file indicate I'm a criminal?" Her nose wrinkled.

"Not always." He grinned at her. Handsome fellow. Not on the same level as the man who'd rescued her, but in some respects more attractive given he wasn't a jerk who accused her of lying.

"Did you question the man who found me?" she asked. When Jacques left her the previous day, he'd planned to visit the property where she'd been found.

"Mr. Laurentian wasn't very helpful, I'm afraid. Claims he found you on the shore. Indications are that you probably washed up there given you were shoeless and without any other items. It is my belief that you were either out for a swim and got into trouble or fell off a boat."

"If I fell off a boat, wouldn't someone have noticed?"

Jacques pursed his lips. "Not always. There are many ships that like to party on the ocean at night."

"So, in other words, we still have no clues." She slumped.

"We will figure this out, mademoiselle. I am doing everything I can to help you regain your identity. Would it be okay if I took your picture and distributed some flyers to the resorts?"

For some reason, the idea of having her image disseminated discomfited. "Can we wait another day or two before we plaster my face everywhere?"

"But of course. Whatever you prefer. Have you given some thought to my offer?"

Apparently, the hospital would have to discharge her the following day. They would have dumped her today if they could have, given the shortage of beds, but her doctor had intervened.

Jacques had kindly offered her a room at his house. She should jump on the chance to leave the hospital with the antiseptic smells and the cries of people in pain. But she hesitated. Jacques was a little too eager for her company.

"I don't know. Perhaps I'll remember who I am before the morning, or someone will come looking for me."

A hint of disappointment flashed on his face— there one moment, gone the next. The wide smile returned. "One can hope. If you change your mind, here is my number." He wrote it down and tore it from a notebook before handing it to her.

"Thank you," she said softly.

He left, and the day ticked by slowly. So very, very slowly. The heat of the afternoon combined with everything else put her to sleep.

She didn't know how long she rested, but she woke when someone entered the room. She kept her eyes closed. Nurses had a tendency to come in and out regularly as they checked on her or swapped out the pitcher of water she kept emptying. She was always so thirsty.

The scuff of a shoe sounded close to the bed. She rolled to her back and opened her eyes as the pillow smashed down on her face.

CHAPTER FOUR

HUGO SPENT part of the morning working out, using the exertion of pumping weights to deal with the restlessness that had gotten even worse over the last few days. Ever since he'd found the woman.

She remained in the hospital, but Francis had discerned that she would be discharged the next day.

"Someone is coming to get her?" he'd asked.

"According to her records, she still hasn't remembered anything, but they're short on beds."

Not his problem. Surely, some kind of charity would provide clothing and a place to stay while things sorted themselves out. It didn't surprise him that they'd kept the story from the media. They didn't want a repeat of the Dominican a while back when all those people died, and the island got blamed.

Then again, Hugo wasn't crazy about tourists. Maybe he should leak the story. He wouldn't, though, because people needed their jobs, and he technically never had to see any visitors with their loud voices and even less subtle clothing.

Given Hugo had business in the city, he dressed in a suit, the linen a light tan, the shirt open-necked. He drove himself and happened to pass by the hospital. Where *she* was staying.

Still not his problem.

So why the fuck did he find himself parking and asking at the desk where the woman with no memory was situated?

The nurses found it very exciting. He wondered what they'd think once they discovered that the woman lied. To his surprise, he found her in a private room on the third floor.

"Is someone paying for her care?" he asked the matron behind the desk. Francis had said she was a ward of the state.

"The superintendent requested it."

Pierrot was showing a lot of interest in the woman. Could be the man was shopping for wife number four.

"Has anyone other than the superintendent been by to see her?"

"*Non.*" The woman lapsed into French.

"Thank you."

He'd not been to the hospital often but could follow signs easily enough. The wing with the private rooms had less humming noise than the other sections of the establishment. As he turned the corner following the directions, he noticed someone in street clothes with a hood pulled over their head slipping into a room. The most interesting thing though was that they were going into *her* room.

Aha. Hugo knew she was faking it, and he'd have proof given he was about to catch her with her accomplice.

He entered the room, expecting to hear them conspiring and trying to hide their guilt.

Instead, he caught the person in the hoodie holding a pillow over the woman's face.

Admittedly unexpected. He barked, "What are you doing?"

The words got a reaction. The person whirled and threw the pillow at Hugo. He rose an arm to deflect the useless missile, only realizing as the person dashed past that it was a delay tactic. He chased the assailant, but not very successfully. It was if he acted in a comedy where nurses kept popping out of rooms, some with trolleys that he narrowly avoided, and patients with IVs tottering into his way. A crowded waiting room meant that he lost sight of the attacker. By the time he reached the door outside, the would-be killer was gone.

This was twice now that he'd saved the mystery redhead. It chilled him to realize that she probably would have suffocated had he not arrived.

Trudging back through the hospital, he discovered Pierrot in the woman's room with that damnable notebook.

The superintendent turned a stern gaze on him, and his hand dropped to the butt of his weapon. "Mr. Laurentian, I'm surprised to see you return to the scene of the crime."

"Fuck off." He didn't even try to temper his tone or language. "It wasn't me trying to smother her. Someone else was in here."

"So you claim. Once again, we are left with your word alone about events. How convenient."

The woman in the bed was the one to rescue him. "Why would he come here to kill me when he had plenty of opportunities to do so at his home?" Her voice was a husky murmur, stronger and less tremulous than the morning he'd found her.

"Because if you died here, it would look as if you succumbed to your injury. At his home, we'd assume murder."

"As if you'd ever find the body," he muttered. Not low enough.

Pierrot opened his mouth to state something that would annoy when the woman smiled. "Exactly my point. Which means, I need to thank you twice for saving me, Mr. Laurentian. Or should I start calling you my hero?"

Two little words that wrenched him and caused him to drawl, "I ain't a hero, miss."

She laughed, an even more throaty sound. "I've seen myself in a mirror. Hardly a miss."

Yet she was too attractive for a ma'am.

Hugo turned his attention from her to Pierrot. "Have you had any luck discovering who she is?"

"Not yet. But, sometimes, these things take time. If she is a guest from out of the country, it might be a few days before a hotel notices the mademoiselle's disappearance."

"Miss. Mademoiselle. I even had a nurse call me the redheaded lady." She sighed. "I need a name."

"In the United States, they often use Jane Doe for those without a proper title," Hugo suggested.

She grimaced. "That makes me feel even more like an invalid. Can't we just guess at a name and see what fits?"

Whereupon, Pierrot began naming off women's names. "Genevieve. Natalie. Patrice." When he faltered, Hugo jumped in and said, "Ariel."

"You would name her after a cartoon mermaid in a movie?" Pierrot scoffed.

Rather than deny it, Hugo shrugged. "Well, she does have the same red hair." Because now that it was dry, he could see the fiery shine of it. It made him wonder if it were natural or bottle-made. His gaze strayed to the sheet covering her lower body. He felt ashamed and returned his attention to her face.

"Named for a princess." She laughed. "You know what, I like it. For now, at least. The doctors say I could get my memories back at any time."

"Then Ariel it is," Hugo declared.

Pierrot frowned at him. "If you weren't trying to kill her, then why are you here?"

Quickly, his mind filtered the reasons he could use. He couldn't say because she wouldn't leave his mind. "Since Ariel was found on my property, I thought I should check and see how she was doing."

"Still can't remember anything. Going to accuse me of lying again?" she said with a finely sculpted brow.

"You have to admit, it's far-fetched. But..." How long would he remain convinced that it was impossible when everything pointed to her having actually lost her identity. "I guess if the doctor says it's true, then I owe you an apology." It lacked sincerity.

She knew it and smirked. "Don't bother. I can see you still have your doubts."

"I'm cautious." He shoved his hands into his pants' pockets. Strangely ill at ease as she accurately read him.

"I for one, believe you," Pierrot declared.

"Big surprise," Hugo muttered. The superintendent had a thing for beautiful women.

Turning her gaze on Pierrot, she asked, "In all the excitement, you never did explain why you returned so soon. Did you get a lead?"

"I thought I'd see if you'd decided to accept my offer."

"What offer?" Hugo volleyed his gaze between them.

"The kind chief of police has offered me a room in his home when the hospital discharges me, but I'm afraid I have to decline. I wouldn't want to give any semblance of impropriety with regards to an obviously well-considered community leader."

Hugo almost burst out laughing at the load of dreck, but Pierrot puffed out his chest. "Who better to ensure your safety?"

He bit his tongue lest he question how Pierrot would guard her virtue. Not his problem.

"It is a kind offer, but I must decline."

"If you change your mind, just call. Now, if you'll excuse me, I must return to the station." Pierrot went to leave, but Hugo detained him. "Leave? What about the man who attacked her?"

"So it was a man?" Pierrot asked. "Because the mademoiselle wasn't sure."

Hugo frowned. He hadn't actually seen the person. Just an impression of size that could have been either sex. "Whoever it was might come back."

"Doubtful."

"She needs police protection," he insisted.

"We are stretched much too thin for what was probably a crime of opportunity. You know how we have problems with the gangs robbing our tourists."

"He wasn't robbing her," Hugo declared through gritted teeth.

"Because you interrupted. Now that he's aware

she's not alone, he'll probably prey on someone else. *Bon jour.*" Pierrot saluted Ariel and then left.

Hugo didn't follow and heard Ariel as she sighed.

"That wasn't exactly reassuring, was it?"

He turned to see her plucking at the worn hospital sheet. "He's probably right. The guy who attacked you will most likely go after someone else next time."

Except it made no sense. Why put a pillow over her face and do nothing else? Hugo prided himself on being a realist. Most attackers would have raped someone as attractive as her, or as Pierrot suggested, robbed. Killing for the hell of it? A knife would have been a quicker method but would make it obvious as homicide. Whereas smothering...they might be able to explain some kind of system failure due to her injury.

"Thank you for the fruit basket."

"What makes you think it was me?"

"You seem like the type." She waved a hand, and he noticed it on a shelf by the window. An impersonal thing with oranges and bananas, some papaya and mango, too. Francis got the one that showed a chocolate bar, still sitting upright, untouched.

Did she not like any of it?

"Are you okay?" The moment he asked, he realized it was a dumb question.

Her wry expression matched the dry tone. "Just peachy, darling." The exaggerated Southern accent rolled off her tongue.

"Sorry, that was insensitive."

"But understandable. What does one say in this situation? Even if I had my memory, I bet you I was never taught how to handle someone with amnesia."

"In the soap operas, they usually go looking for clues to find a trail to the past."

That brought a husky chuckle. "You want us to pull a Fred and Daphne, we'll need a van and a dog."

Hugo couldn't help but grin. "*Scooby-Doo* references. I think we just got our first clue."

Her cheeks pinked. "I think I just dated myself."

"Not really. After all, the gang's been around for a few decades now."

"Nineteen seventy-four to be exact." Her eyes widened. "How the heck do I know something obscure like that, but not my bra size?"

"Thirty-six C."

She blinked. "I don't know if I should be disturbed that you've been eyeing my chest or curious about the fact that it sounds right."

He rolled his shoulders. "It's a matter of observation and experience."

"How would I go about looking for clues?" she asked. "I have nothing on me."

"Which is interesting, because resorts tend to bracelet their guests. At least the all-inclusive ones do—"

"It could have fallen off," she interrupted. "Soaked and worn off."

"They're made to go in the water. They don't disintegrate or tear. Takes scissors or a knife to remove them."

"I don't suppose you found one on the beach with me."

He shook his head. "I didn't see one. And Pierrot never mentioned anything."

"That narrows the search. I just need to start contacting places that don't have bracelets."

"Which still number in the dozens for this area."

"Oh." Her lips turned down, and he felt inexplicably annoyed with himself for putting the frown there. Would it kill him to give her a little chunk of hope?

"You should go on the local news and ask for help. Even if the tourists don't watch it much, the locals do. Someone might recognize you from somewhere."

She shook her head immediately. "I don't think I could stand to have my face plastered everywhere. And what if someone fake tries to claim me."

"Why would anyone do that?" he asked in genuine confusion.

"I think I saw that in a movie." She frowned. "It was an action flick with an all-girl cast. Kind of Charlie's Angels-ish."

"I will be sure to avoid it. If you're not going to put yourself out there, then I don't know how you'll get your next clue."

She rolled her shoulders. "Pierrot is running my fingerprints. Maybe I shoplifted somewhere when I was younger, and they'll be able to identify me."

"Maybe you're wanted for mass murder, and they'll start the process to extradite you."

She blinked.

He smiled. "You aren't the only one who can toss out far-fetched theories."

That brought a responding grin. "Both options are more exciting than the possibility I'm just some boring woman here on holiday going back to some mundane job and life."

"Nothing wrong with being ordinary."

"But why settle when you could strive for extraordinary?"

That made him chuckle. "Good point. Now, did I hear correctly? Are the doctors actually discharging you?"

Her shoulders rolled, and one slipped free of the loose gown she wore. "Technically, other than the memory thing, there is nothing wrong with me."

He frowned. "That can't be right. You suffered a head wound."

"Which is healing. Staying here won't hasten it, and they need this bed."

Someone really needed to either add on or build a new hospital. "You said no to going with Pierrot. I assume you have a plan."

"Not really. I was hoping I could beg some real clothes from the staff and then kind of wander around and see if I remember anything."

"That is the stupidest plan ever," he blurted.

She shrugged. "Kind of the only thing I *can* do."

"With nowhere to sleep? What will you eat? It's not safe for you." The claim might have been what prompted his next words. "You'll stay with me."

Her reaction?

Laughter.

"What's so funny?" he growled.

"You, faking politeness for my sake."

His brows drew together. "How is offering you a place to stay polite?"

"Because you obviously feel some kind of moral obligation given you've saved me twice."

"I hate to break it to you, but I don't owe you anything."

Her brow angled on one side. "Then why are you trying to provide me with a roof over my head? You could easily walk away. Right now. And never look back. I am nothing to you."

She was well-spoken with a slight Southern drawl. American, he'd wager. "I could walk away, but then again, I have a big house."

"Is it really big enough given you don't even like me?"

"I wouldn't say that exactly." He was starting to find the woman very fascinating: her speech, her mannerisms, the obvious intelligence in her slamming body.

She rolled her eyes. "You accused me of being a conniving liar trying to extort you."

"Then prove me wrong." He couldn't have said why he insisted, except that he kept seeing that pillow holding her down. Her body limp on the beach. The woman obviously needed a keeper.

Why was he volunteering, though?

"You don't have to help me." Said softly, and he knew she meant it.

"I know. But here's the thing, you have nowhere to go. Not until you regain your memory, that is. Which means, no money for a hotel or food. And before you mention a shelter, you wouldn't last a day in one of them. I, on the other hand, have quite a few empty rooms. A cook who thinks he's feeding an army every night, not to mention security in case this wasn't just a crime of happenstance."

She appeared thoughtful. But not about his offer.

"I wonder how they knew that the extra pillow would be on that chair?" She eyed the currently empty seat.

"Who left it there?"

"The nurse who was doing the bedding forgot it when she was called away for some kind of emergency."

"Where did the pillow go?" Hugo asked.

"I don't know. I was too busy trying to breath to notice."

Perhaps she didn't recollect, but Hugo recalled it being flung at him. It should have been on the floor, yet wasn't.

"Who else has been in here?"

"Right after you chased the killer off, the nurse ran in, followed by the police chief."

"Perhaps they took the pillow."

She shrugged. "Maybe. I don't really care about the damned thing. I'm more interested in the fact that someone tried to smother me." She eyed the door nervously.

"Most likely a crime of circumstance."

"Is it? Seems like a big coincidence given I almost drowned," she grumbled.

He couldn't blame her suspicion. "If the two events are related, then even more reason for you to go somewhere more secure like my place." Look at him, begging the woman to come. What was wrong with him? Maybe *he* should be seeing a doctor. Could be they had a pill to cure him of this crazy affliction.

"It's too generous, especially since I don't know if I can repay you."

He snorted. "I can afford it, don't worry. Not asking for payment. I don't even know why I'm offering."

Those vivid blue eyes met his and held his gaze. "Because, despite what you keep saying, you're obviously a hero. A savior of damsels in distress. I accept, Mr. Laurentian."

There she went, calling him something he wasn't again. He was known to be ruthless. "How did you

47

know my name?" He frowned, suspicion rearing its head.

Her laughter mocked. "Because Jacques told me."

"Jacques, is it?" He couldn't explain the sudden flare of heat. He just knew he didn't like her familiarity with the superintendent.

"Now, Mr. Laurentian, don't be angry. It was he who insisted."

"Don't call me that." She'd said it herself, Hugo was the one who'd saved her twice. And yet, Pierrot got those lips saying his name, not Hugo's.

"What would you like me to call you?" Her gaze became transfixed on his.

"Hugo."

"Sounds French."

"Because I am. And before you ask me, no, I will not speak French for your entertainment." A common demand by Americans who found it exotic.

"I don't need you to speak it because I apparently do, as well. Along with Spanish and Italian."

"That's a lot of languages."

"Why would I know so many? Am I a flight attendant?" Her expression brightened. "Maybe I travel around the world."

"You could be a nanny, too."

Her smile turned hard. "That was sexist."

"How is a nanny sexist?"

"Assuming an educated woman would be teaching the children of the wealthy."

"Because you'd never survive teaching anywhere else." Not with her fine features.

"And now you've accused me of being weak."

"Are you going to find insult in everything I say?"

She cocked her head. "If you keep doing it, yes. Would you like to rescind the invitation?"

"First off, when I said 'nanny,' I didn't mean the old spinster type. You are definitely in your prime. And sexy. Would you have preferred I said '*librarian*?'"

"And still not making a case for not being a misogynist."

"I will not apologize for finding you attractive. And before you think this is me trying to proposition you, it should be clear that I am not, and I will not ever have any kind of relations with you."

"That was blunt."

"Experience has taught me that sometimes it's best."

"In that case, I am not sleeping with you either. And not just because you're obviously a chauvinist."

He restrained himself from yelling, but she really was provoking him. "What other reason could there be?" he said with exaggerated sarcasm.

"I don't know who I am or who I'm with. Duh."

If she was faking the amnesia, she was doing a fine job of covering it. "Now that we've clarified that, I would also ask that you not advertise your presence in my home."

"Protecting your reputation with the ladies." She nodded.

"I don't date."

"Is it because your wife wouldn't like it?"

"Are you trying to find out if I'm single?" he countered.

He would have liked to believe the flush in her cheeks, but surely, a woman of her years no longer felt heated embarrassment.

"I have no interest in you. Just recovering my memories."

"And I might be able to help with that. I've got access to things Pierrot doesn't."

"You'd help me? Why?"

"Weren't you the one who said I had a hero complex?"

She tilted her head. "In this case, I think it's more the feline one. Curiosity."

A smile tugged his lips. "Can you blame me? By helping me sate my need, we solve your dilemma."

"In that case, I accept." She held out her hand, and he looked at it a moment before taking it in his, his grip engulfing hers. He noticed the fine bone structure, the heat of her skin, and a jolt of awareness zinged through him.

He dropped her hand quickly and fled, saying, "I'm going to see what's needed to get you discharged." And maybe ask for a mental evaluation while he was at it.

CHAPTER FIVE

AN HOUR LATER, sitting in the passenger seat of an air-conditioned luxury car, Ariel didn't know why Hugo looked so sour. He was the one who'd offered her a place to stay, practically begged her, and then made all the arrangements: getting her discharged and acquiring clothes for her instead of the bathing suit she'd arrived in.

All that effort, and now he sat across from her in the driver's seat, ignoring her. Understandable when he drove and needed to pay attention, but he never looked at her once. Didn't say a single word.

Then again, she didn't either.

Confusion mixed with the lingering pain in her head and made it so she didn't want to think. She just stared blankly out the window at a tropical paradise that didn't seem familiar at all. Not to mention the heat. She'd wilted the moment she left the hospital, lending credence to the theory that she was a tourist. Surely a citizen of the islands wouldn't melt.

The set of gates slowed the smooth ride, the purr of the motor barely noticeable. He didn't have to signal for the metal portal to slide open, allowing them entrance. Right inside, she saw a jungle, dense foliage lining a fat but single-lane drive.

"Where are you taking me?" she asked.

"The house."

"Your house?" She didn't recall much of it, her head had been so fuzzy at the time.

"Where else?" He sounded almost mocking.

"I thought you'd stick me out of the way in a cabana or something."

"Can't keep an eye on you if you're not close by. Your doctor insisted."

Ariel grimaced. "I feel fine." Was even discharged with a clean bill of health, and yet the doctor with her hair in a wavy halo and a bright smile had insisted that Ariel be monitored.

"Indulge me, then. If you die while in my custody, Pierrot will make my life difficult."

"Glad to see it's all about you."

"Perhaps not the hero you thought, eh?" he said.

For all his gruff and sometimes rude remarks, he was going out of his way. Only one way to handle him. "I am grateful that you're doing this."

Just like the first time she'd said it, Hugo shut up. Interesting that gratitude disarmed him. As if she would say *"no"* to his offer. He could not only provide better meals, but he also had the means to dig a little deeper and faster than the police.

Having seen what passed as food, and not having any funds, hunger did motivate her acceptance, as did the idea of security. There was something frightening about not knowing who she was. About wondering if perhaps her stint in the ocean weren't an accident but something more nefarious.

With no past to guide her, she could be anyone. The wife of a rich billionaire who didn't want to pay for a divorce. A high-powered executive with jealous competition. For all she knew, she was a secret spy.

The very thought made her almost laugh. Given how she'd frozen when that pillow was shoved over her face, she obviously didn't have the kind of stoic nerve needed to fight.

The house came into view, although the term *house* really seemed inadequate. Mansion came to mind, perhaps even luxury palace given how it sprawled. The exterior appeared made of smooth, white concrete, formed intricately into a thing of beauty. The frames around the windows were carved like scalloped shells. The roof was heavy clay tile. The shrubbery had a wildness to it that she'd wager was actually cultivated, with flowering vines climbing strategically placed trellises and wrapping around a few stone columns.

A paradise that seemed much too big for a man alone.

"How many people live here with you?" she asked. Did he have a partner? Kids?

"It's just me." A terse reply.

"I wonder if I have a family," she mused aloud. She didn't mention how she kept picturing a little boy. Flying backwards and hitting a wall. She flinched each time and couldn't help but wonder if it was a memory, and if so, was she the one who'd hit the child? As if her mind couldn't bear for her to remember, it never showed her more than that single moment.

"If you have family, then they will get worried and come looking," he remarked as he pulled to a stop. He exited the vehicle and was around it, opening her door for her, by the time she'd unclipped the belt. He even extended a hand to help her out of the low-slung sports car.

A gentlemanly thing to do, yet the moment she stood beside him, he snatched his hand away as if she had the plague.

The door opened, and a thickset man appeared, wearing a loose, navy-blue, button-up shirt over khaki shorts, his feet bare. His dark hair was cut short, and his tanned features indicated a possible Polynesian heritage. He was older than Hugo, probably by about ten years.

Hugo swept a hand in his direction. "This is Gerome. My everything guy."

"Ma'am." He offered a slight tilt of his head.

She reached out her hand. "Hi, I'm Ariel."

At the questioning look directed at his employer, Hugo shook his head. "The name she chose since she can't remember her own."

"I'm sure with some rest, it will return to you, ma'am."

"Please, just Ariel." She followed Gerome inside, conscious that Hugo was at her back. For some reason, it discomfited. Stuck between them with no escape.

Why would she be so worried? She'd chosen to come.

Sunshine shone through the skylight overhead in the vestibule, drawing attention to the crushed coral floor glossed over with a hard finish. The walls appeared to be smoothed concrete, painted an ivory that provided a backdrop to the brilliant blooms filling the vases.

On either side of the entranceway stood double doors, the wood of them darkly varnished. They were closed, hiding what lay on the other side.

"Did you prepare a room for her?" Hugo asked.

"Yes."

"Then I'll leave you to show her." Hugo didn't even glance her way as he strode to a closed door and disappeared behind it.

Abrupt, and yet she found herself less tense already.

Gerome caught her watching. "That's the boss's

office. Consider it off-limits unless you want to get reamed out."

"I think I'll pass." Her nose wrinkled.

"Good plan. He can be quite loud about it. Other than the office, there isn't much space you can't check out. Living room, dining, kitchen, game room, television room, library."

"Do guests receive a map?"

The big man grinned at her. "It's hard to get lost. Main floor has one long hall. And the second floor is just bedrooms."

"So, I'll be sleeping upstairs?"

"That's for family. We're going this way," Gerome advised as he skirted a table in the center of the space. Once past the giant vase on it, she noted a corridor led them deeper into the house before connecting to a long hall that went left and right, lined in windows.

"Have you worked for Mr. Laurentian a long time?" she asked.

"Long enough."

Not really an answer. "I don't get the impression he's very social."

Gerome snorted. "He's not, which is why I was kind of surprised he brought you home."

"It's only because he's got a hero complex."

The remark for some reason caused Gerome to choke. "Don't ever tell him that."

"I did, and he didn't correct me."

"Probably stunned," Gerome mumbled.

"I don't think he likes me very much," she admitted.

"He don't like many people." The growl sounded more like a warning.

As they walked along the corridor lined with windows that overlooked the ocean and a backyard oasis, they passed the television room Gerome had mentioned, plus one set up as a spa with massage tables. "This place seems too big for a guy who doesn't like to socialize."

"There was a time he thought he'd settle down."

"And?"

Gerome rolled his shoulders. "It didn't work out, but he liked the property." At the very end of the hall, he stopped in front of a door, stained dark like all the others. "Here's your room." He swung it open, but rather than look inside, she glanced at the camera parked across from it, the small, glass eye watching. She'd noticed the dome mounts dotting their path, an excessive amount of them she thought, especially inside. She wouldn't complain, though. Hugo had promised security.

"The room has its own bathroom and a walk-in closet."

She followed Gerome in, stating, "I don't have any clothes."

"Yes, you do. The boss had some stores deliver things in your size."

"Of course, he did, despite not knowing what I like to wear."

"Don't be so sure of that. The boss is observant."

"The boss is a chicken who escaped me." She glanced down the hall but didn't see him.

"He's a busy man. As am I. So, let's get this over with." Gerome swept a hand to encompass the room. "Fresh linens on the bed, there are towels and toiletries in the washroom." He jabbed a finger at a phone on the nightstand. "If you need anything—food, aspirin, something not in this room—just hit zero, and you'll be in touch with either me or whoever else is on call."

"Part of being Hugo's everything guy?"

"And now yours, for the moment."

"I can take care of myself."

"I'm sure you can, but I do make good muscle. I hear you had a spot of trouble at the hospital."

Her lips pulled down. "The police chief seemed to think it was an isolated incident."

"What do you think?"

She shrugged. "That I don't understand anything right now."

"Then it's a good thing you're here. We'll keep you safe," Gerome promised.

He left, and she was alone in a room of luxury. She kicked off her sandals, and her toes sank into the plush carpet by the bed. She flopped onto the mattress and sighed.

Much better than the hospital. Still, she couldn't

relax. The sense of familiarity had only increased after meeting Gerome. His face seemed familiar. Parts of the house made her feel as if she suffered déjà vu.

Yet Hugo claimed they'd never met. Why would he lie?

Perhaps they *had* met. Maybe they were even friends. Or worse, lovers. What if the lump on her head wasn't an accident but something intentional, and he was at fault?

If that were the case, she'd just delivered herself to him and made it easy for him to eliminate her.

Except...that didn't make much sense. He'd interrupted whoever had tried to suffocate her. She'd seen two men in the room before they bolted.

And again, why call the ambulance if he wanted to get rid of her?

She walked to the closet and opened it to see a decent assortment of clothes. More than she would need for a few days.

She stroked her fingers over the fine fabrics and noticed the tags still on every single item. Not a hand-me-down. Not a discard from an ex-girlfriend or mistress.

There were comfortable things like yoga sets and athletic wear, to light summer pieces, to even some fancier evening wear. A dark blue sheath gown tucked on one hip and low-cut in both front and back.

Much too sexy.

She itched to put it on, but instead, turned from

the closet to eye the rest of the room. The patio door led to the yard, the garden outside a wild riot of color and smells. She decided to explore.

It didn't take long for fatigue to make her yawn. Twilight fell, and she wandered back to her room to find a tray of food.

A hearty soup, and some fruit, cheese, and bread. She fell asleep on the bed, face-first on the covers, and didn't wake until she felt the slide of something over her leg.

Immediately, she came awake, knowing that she wasn't alone. All of a sudden, Hugo's insistence on her coming here made sense. He'd lied. He did want to sleep with her.

"I said no!" She kicked and rolled, fumbling for a lamp. When it lit, she blinked for a moment. Then her lips rounded into a giant O of surprise as the snake hissed and lunged.

CHAPTER SIX

THE SCREAM COULD ONLY BE from one person, and Hugo responded immediately, racing back across the pool patio, the echo of the shout dying without being repeated.

His bare feet pounded on the concrete decking of his pool then down the cobbled path to the far end of his house. He'd placed her there to keep her out of sight, and now cursed the choice given the distance.

A light shone from her patio doors when he arrived, huffing only slightly. He stepped aside as Gerome exited, hand outstretched, serpentine body dangling from it.

"That's a big one," Hugo remarked as his man marched past.

"Miss Ariel left her door open, and it must have slid in."

"I did not." Hugo heard her shout from inside.

He followed the voice. "Well, it certainly didn't magically appear in your room."

"I agree. Someone put it there."

He arched a brow. "You think someone snuck onto the property, evading my security, to slip a snake into your room."

"Yes."

"Why?"

"So it would bite me, and I'd die."

"I have an antidote."

"Which you can only administer if you know I'm poisoned. But what if I hadn't yelled for help?"

"Then after it bit you, you probably had about fifteen minutes before things started getting rough."

"It could have strangled me to death in that time."

"You're thinking of a different snake."

"I know about snakes," she hissed.

So did he, and those big ones she spoke of didn't live in the populated areas, but in the jungle mountains. Still...

"Would you like to change rooms?"

"I don't know." She flopped onto the bed, wearing only a short, silken gown that barely hit her mid-thigh.

"How about I lock the patio door and check the room for critters?"

"What if they come in person to kill me next time?"

"They'd have to break the glass, and that would set off alarms."

"Alarms won't save me if the attacker's got a knife." She hugged a pillow to her chest. "I'm being crazy, aren't I?"

"A little."

"It's terrifying not knowing anything," she admitted.

He sat on the edge of the bed and hesitated with his hand over her back. Could he touch and offer comfort? He abstained and would have sworn she shriveled a little more.

"This was probably just an accident." He stood and locked the patio door before doing a thorough job of searching the space. Under the bed, dressers, in the closet, the bathroom.

When he returned, he found her lying on her back under the covers, watching him. "All clear," Hugo announced.

"Thank you." She didn't look relaxed.

He returned to the bed and sat down. "Want me to stay while you fall asleep again?"

"Shouldn't you be sleeping?" she asked, turning on her side.

"I don't sleep so good anymore."

"Why?"

"Too many reasons to list."

"I'm afraid to close my eyes. What if I lose more of myself every time I do?"

"You need rest."

"Says the man who doesn't sleep."

"Move over."

"Why?"

"If you're going to yap, then I'm getting comfortable."

"You'll really stay?"

He found himself replying softly, "Yeah."

She rolled to her back and shuffled over. He stretched out beside her, on top of the covers but somehow still very aware of her.

"How old are you?" she asked.

"Isn't that question forbidden?"

"Only if you ask a woman. Men are distinguished with age."

He snorted. "Not really. I'm forty-nine."

"I think I'm in my forties. I am definitely not in my thirties."

"You could be a hot fifty!"

She jabbed him, and he found himself guffawing. "Hey, I called it hot."

"Might as well call me a cougar," she grumbled.

"You do know cougar means sexy, too?"

"Are you flirting with me?"

"Never," he lied as he flirted.

"So, if I'm a cougar, I guess that makes you a silver fox."

"I don't have enough gray for that."

"Still counts." She'd rolled to her side, her back to him, and he found himself tilting, not touching her but noticing the shape of her, the rise and fall of her chest as she breathed.

"Go to sleep," he said a little more roughly than intended.

"Why do you hate me?"

"I don't hate you."

"You sound angry half the time when you talk to me."

"Maybe that's just my personality."

"Hmm." She snuggled closer, her voice faint. She didn't say anything further. He remained still, conscious of her almost touching him. Her breathing soft and even.

Normal? How would he know?

He watched her, and the next thing he knew, a slant of dawning light woke him.

Woke. Him.

He'd slept. The whole damned night through until dawn.

How?

He looked to see Ariel snuggled against his chest, her hair a soft red cloud for his chin. He'd not just slept, he'd cuddled.

Hugo fled that bed as if someone had set it on fire.

INTERLUDE: PRE-WEDDING BRUNCH

T-MINUS FOUR DAYS until the wedding.

Audrey—code name Frenemy Mom—met up with the other moms, sans their partners, for brunch. The best meal of the day. It had the yummies of breakfast with some of the more solid carbs from a lunch. With a bun in the oven, she found herself craving a wider variety. Poor Mason, her boyfriend, received the news of the impending child via vomit. To his credit rather than be grossed out, he'd asked, "Should I ask why I'm wearing pickles and jellybeans?"

She'd replied, "Pregnancy hormones." And what did the idiot do with the news? Told everyone at the Bad Boy Inc. office meaning she got treated like some kind of delicate princess and got offered donuts every time she showed up to meet him.

Audrey eyed the buffet, marking what she wanted then filled a plate to the brim, meaning she had to put the extra bacon on a second one. She joined the others and noticed one chair was conspicuously empty. "Has anyone seen Meredith?"

"I was going to ask the same thing," Tanya said. "I haven't seen her since I got here."

"Probably going over every last-minute detail. The woman is a wedding taskmaster." Carla groaned. "Do you know how many times she came to make me try on the dress? And she kept warning me not to overeat, for fear I might split a seam."

"I bet it was almost as many times as she made us try on our bridesmaids' gowns," Audrey grumbled. She'd had hers loosened, given her belly was already starting to swell. Meaning she'd have to tell Mother she was no longer fit for field duty. Good thing she could still work via computer.

"Meredith won't be joining us for brunch or tonight's entertainment," Mother stated, placing a napkin in her lap.

"Oh no, is she okay? Did she get food poisoning?" Tanya exclaimed.

Portia, the always-prepared mom of the group, jumped in. "I have remedies for diarrhea and upset stomach."

"She's not sick, just a tad occupied at the moment." Mother took a bite of her fruit salad.

Audrey eyed their handler suspiciously. "Occupied how, exactly?"

Louisa made a face. "I don't need details if it's

another of her boy toys." Meredith liked men. Too much at times.

"Other matters require her attention at the moment."

Which could only mean one thing. "Holy crap. You sent her on a mission."

Carla cursed. "You do realize she's planning my wedding?"

"Your wedding will be fine. You know how organized she is. Everything has already been taken care of."

Carla wasn't placated. "She's supposed to be my bridesmaid."

"She'll be back in time for the ceremony."

But the Killer Moms, who so rarely all got together like this, wouldn't let Mother off the hook so easily.

"Is she still on the island?"

"Does she need backup?"

"Pass the jam."

Only Mother appeared unperturbed.

Carla slammed a hand on the table. "Enough of the evasion. What have you done with Meredith?"

"Nothing. She's on a mission. Nothing too dangerous. I actually expected her to conduct it while staying on the resort, but she appears to have decided to get close to the target."

"Meaning he must be cute," Audrey declared before biting into her toast.

Meredith could be a bit of a maneater. Sex was

something she had no problem with. Intimacy, though... Like the rest of the mothers, she had trust issues.

Personally, Audrey thought she just needed to meet the right person. That's what it had taken for Audrey, and now Carla. She'd met Philip, and after a tumultuous start, had never been happier, even if she'd more or less retired.

But not working for KM anymore, the agency that had helped drag her and her son out of an impossible situation, didn't mean those ties with the women she'd bonded with broke. They remained as strong as ever. Which was why Mother's explanation niggled.

"She wouldn't abandon me this close to the wedding." Meredith wouldn't do that knowing how Carla's nerves would be shot. Audrey had spent time with Carla, heard her friend hyperventilating as she paced the resort bedroom.

"I'm getting married." She fluttered her hands.

"It's going to be amazing!" Audrey enthused.

"Will it? I never imagined this day happening. Ever."

Carla had spent so long being tough and taking care of Nico, that she'd not imagined she had room in her heart for anyone else.

Audrey had spent a bunch of time running scared herself. But now with Mason, she could do anything.

After the baby was born.

She put a hand on her stomach.

"Meredith hasn't abandoned you. I assure you, she'll be back in plenty of time to soothe your anxiety. Speaking of which, I have Ativan," Mother offered, pointing to her purse.

Carla scowled. "I don't need drugs."

"But you will need copious amounts of alcohol tonight," Tanya, the usually staid member of their group stated. She'd loosened up quite a bit since meeting Devon on a mission. Happiness suited her, and she needed to make up for lost fun times.

"Do we have to do a bachelorette?" Carla groaned. "I swear, if anyone hires strippers..."

"Don't blame us if they show up. Blame Meredith."

"Think she'll slip out to join us?" Audrey asked. Things really were more fun with the Southern belle.

"I'm sure you can all manage to get drunk on your own. Now, can we be done? Or do I have to shoot all of you?"

Audrey chose to eat some bacon but exchanged a glance with the other mothers. Only they never had a chance to act. As if Mother conspired against them, they were kept apart with various tasks until it was time to go out and party.

Until they finally ditched Mother.

Carla waited while they all gathered on the rooftop balcony before saying, "Something doesn't feel right. I think we need to find Meredith."

"You heard Mother. She's fine and will be back soon. In the meantime..." It was Portia who grinned mischievously as she opened her bag and pulled out a headband. It said *bride* and had pink antennae that ended in tiny penises.

The wide eyes on Carla's face were worth it. "I am not wearing that."

More of them emerged.

They all wore the penis headbands and spent the day giggling. But it seemed wrong without Meredith.

CHAPTER EIGHT

HUGO HAD BEEN on edge ever since he woke next to Ariel. He'd bolted from her room and immediately stripped and showered.

Not because he felt dirty. On the contrary. He felt energized and aware. The scent of Ariel clung to him, and he enjoyed it too much.

He had to scrub it off. Scour her from his skin and mind. Irrational, yes, but he'd finally reached an age and time in his life where he just wasn't going to try anymore. He wasn't meant to be with a woman. They lied. They put on airs. And none pretended more than the one in his guest bedroom.

How had she made him sleep? Could it be a drug?

He spent the day in his office after that, faking work. Mostly trying to find new ways to discover who his guest really was.

Hugo drummed his fingers on his desk and

frowned at the report on his screen. A report with nothing in it. Which bothered him because he'd not been exaggerating when he claimed that he had better resources than Pierrot. He could access things the police couldn't. He'd run her fingerprints against every known database that carried them. Done a search on her appearance, as well. Even omitting the red hair in case it wasn't natural. Nothing. She'd not committed a crime that she was ever arrested for. Hadn't been declared missing by anyone.

Ariel appeared to be just as she claimed. An innocent woman who'd suffered an accident and couldn't remember her past. She never fell out of character. He should know, he watched, not in person but remotely. The only place she didn't have a camera monitoring her was in the bathroom. But given that she'd arrived with nothing, he highly doubted she could magic herself a phone and call anyone.

Despite monitoring for heightened interest in the property or intruders, there'd been nothing since her arrival—if he ignored the snake, which he still wasn't sure about. Given her abrupt appearance on his beach, though, he ordered even more cameras to watch the perimeter.

With the click of a button, the report on the screen changed to the video feed on the pool patio. His guest sat in the shade by the pool, reading, though not a fictional romance novel or some kind of thriller. She'd asked for newspapers, hoping the headlines would jar her memories.

All media did for Hugo was give him a headache. The truth in news reporting had gone from a neutral stance that stuck to the facts to a complicated mix of supposition with bits taken out of context in many cases to sensationalize or push a particular opinion. He missed the days when things were reported straight with no embellishment.

His phone rang, and he noted the unknown number. "Allo." The French equivalent of *hello* always slipped past his lips when he answered, even though he'd moved from his home country a long time ago. The warrants for his arrest at the time might have hastened that departure.

"I hear you're thinking of installing an infinity hot tub. Any way I can finagle an invitation?"

Recognizing the voice, he leaned back in his seat. "No need for code. The line is secure."

"Good." The joviality turned businesslike. "Sorry to call out of the blue, but I saw something that concerns you."

"Must be serious since you called me direct." Usually, they went through a layer of online shells to exchange messages of import.

"I didn't want to waste time. A hit has been put out on you."

"Really? I'm surprised, considering what happened

the last time." A man in his position made enemies. Taking care of them was just par for the course.

"Short memories. You've been ruffling feathers again."

Hugo knew his friend couldn't see his cold smile as he replied, "It is what I do best. What details can you give me?" He kept watching the video feed of the woman reading by his pool. Wearing the same swim-suit he'd found her in, but despite the heat outside, she'd yet to go for a swim.

"The information is sparse. Anonymously posted. Few conditions attached." Meaning the person didn't care if the death appeared natural or not. "You dead, in exchange for ten million."

He whistled. "Someone isn't messing around." Nice to know he was worth a hefty chunk. "And no idea who put out the hit?"

"Haven't a clue. Whoever it is hid their tracks."

Not for long. He'd sic Gerome on them, right after Gerome freaked out for not having caught the dark web hit on Hugo's life first. "Have they already found a taker?"

"Yes. More than one, actually. It was posted as an open job, first to prove they did the deed gets the big bucks."

"A free-for-all?" He snorted. "Great."

"Thought you should know so you can increase security."

"Already did." He didn't mention that he'd done it for Ariel. "Thanks for the heads-up."

He hung up and pondered the sudden hit on his life and the mystery woman. Coincidence? He didn't believe in those. He wondered how far she'd take the charade.

He was more eager than expected to find out.

Placing a call to Francis, he relayed what he knew.

There was some predictable swearing, and then a promise. "I will find out who placed the bounty. And then take that money from them with interest."

If anyone could do it, Francis could.

"Anything on the mystery lady?"

"Not yet. I've got a subroutine with her image going through airport arrival footage, but it will take a while."

"And it won't help if she was on a cruise line or a private charter." She had the look of someone affluent. The idea that she'd fallen off a yacht was a good one.

"Did you get the strand of hair yet for a DNA filter?"

"No." Hugo didn't mention that he *could* have. Surely, the pillow they'd shared would have had more than a few. "I'll send Gerome in there to grab some."

"Are you sure you shouldn't put her in a hotel? Especially given the bounty on your head?"

Having her nearby put her at risk, and yet, putting her far away might be just as dangerous. He'd saved her from three accidents now. Either it was an elaborate ruse to make him feel responsible for her, or she genuinely should fear for her life.

"I'll handle any threats that come knocking."

A bold statement, given he still stared at the video feed of her lying by the pool. A beautiful woman. A gorgeous liar.

If he went in with his eyes open, she had no power over him.

He would get no answers staying away. That was the excuse he used to justify joining her by the pool a moment later.

CHAPTER NINE

HUGO STOOD BY HER SEAT—LOOMED, actually. Casting a shadow over her, not that Ariel sat in the sun. She'd started in the shade, and a good thing too, considering she turned pink even out of direct UV rays. Perhaps her inability to tolerate daylight explained her nocturnal swim. She should have known with the red hair that she'd burn easily in the sun.

He, on the other hand, bronzed like a god. Was built like one, too.

In his forties at least, Hugo kept fit, the tone of his body firm without the paunch other men sometimes developed with age—another strange thing she knew but couldn't explain. He was broad through the shoulder, thick in the arms. His hips were lean, his man parts encased in tight-fitting black undershorts that left nothing to the imagination.

"I think you forgot to put on your pants," she

remarked, turning her gaze to his face rather than his crotch.

"Not forgotten, given I don't usually swim in them."

"Do you always parade around in your underpants or is this just for my benefit?" she asked, her tone a little frosty. He'd spent the night with her, cradling her close. But he'd fled as she slept, ignoring her until now when he showed up wearing practically nothing. Did he think she would be so grateful at his kindness that she'd spread her legs for him?

"What are you talking about? These are swim shorts."

"Did you get them a few sizes too small?"

"Small isn't a word usually used to describe me," he drawled.

The reminder drew her gaze. She tried not to stare but then couldn't help it because he reacted, started to thicken, the size of him impressive.

He dragged the towel from his shoulder and dangled it in front.

Modesty now? A tad too late. How dare he conceal the view? Surely, looking was allowed.

Perhaps she shouldn't be too hasty. Maybe a good shagging was precisely what she needed. No. No sex. No flirting. She couldn't get involved with anyone until she knew her status.

"You going to join me for a swim?" he asked,

distracting her from the urge to yank the towel from him.

Swim, not screw. Definitely not on her list of things she wanted to do. "No, thanks. I'm afraid I'll burn if I do."

"I'm sure we can wrangle some sunscreen for that."

"Gerome already brought me some and told me to wear it. More like *ordered,* and I'm pretty sure he would have held me down and slathered it on himself if I didn't agree."

"Gerome can have a,"—he cleared his throat—"certain overprotectiveness regarding those he considers his charges."

"Protecting me from skin cancer. I guess I should be more grateful. But it feels greasy," she said with a grimace, holding out her arm.

"That means it's guarding like it's supposed to."

She reached for the bottle and offered it. "You should probably use some, too. That sun is vicious."

"No need." His teeth flashed as he laughed. "I live for this kind of weather."

He walked off; the back of him just as nice as the front. Given her situation, it seemed all kinds of wrong to lust after him. What if she were married or in a committed relationship? It would still be cheating if she didn't remember.

She glanced at her left hand. No tan line indicating a ring had been there. But that didn't mean anything.

A splash of water caught her attention, and from

the ripple, she saw his body streaking underwater, powerful flexes of his legs and strong pulls of his arms bringing him almost the length of the pool before he surfaced at the far end.

She leaned back and pretended interest in the tablet in her lap. Asking for newspapers was met with chuckles from the butler, Gerome. Apparently, Mr. Laurentian did his part to not pollute the environment. He banned the purchase of single-use bottles and would only buy alcohol that came in the returnable kind. Bought his produce fresh from the market. No canned goods.

That meant no actual newspapers but something better, a tablet with a web browser and an internet connection.

The first thing she'd done was to do a search for news of a missing woman in the Bahamas.

Lots of hits on the search engine—try nine million four hundred and forty thousand returns on that criteria—but nothing in the previous few days or even the last month. How far back should she look? She had no idea how long she'd been missing. When the searches returned nothing of use, she glanced at the world news, seeing if any of the shock headlines jolted anything loose.

A politician caught in a scandal.

Murmurs of war.

Even more of peace.

Celebrity scandal.

All of it seemed familiar and yet not at the same time. Odd how her mind picked what it chose to recall.

Like she remembered that she hated cinnamon on anything, so when Gerome offered her some for her waffle that morning, she had practically thrown herself over it instead of saying a polite, "*no*."

Triggered by a spice. But she couldn't have said why.

Her gaze rose from the tablet in time to see her host doing another lap, choosing to swim on the surface now with long strokes and flutter kicks. Did she know how to swim? The bathing suit implied that she did, but what if she jumped into the pool and sank? Pierrot had mentioned the possibility that she'd fallen off a boat, meaning it was possible she couldn't swim.

It would be a farce of epic proportions if she were to drown in a backyard pool after everything she'd survived.

Ariel never even realized how long she stared until Hugo resurfaced on his return lap, a wet god streaming water from his flesh as he used his hands on the edge of the pool to hoist himself up. From this angle, he looked bare below the waist. That V really wanted her to follow it down.

"You sure you won't join me?" He must be part devil, given how he tempted.

She admitted her concern. "What if I can't swim?"

"Then stand up, and you won't drown." He pushed

from the edge and stood in the pool, showing the water hitting him at mid-chest.

Ariel felt the heat in her cheeks. Way to look stupid at her age. "I don't know if I should."

"Come on, the water is nice. Maybe you'll remember something if you submerge yourself."

A good point, and she was being a coward. Was the old her scared of trying things? Or adventurous? Did it matter? She could choose to be however she liked.

And she'd like to be the type of person who at least tried. She put down the tablet and rose, the bathing suit she wore her own, the wrap something found in the closet, presumably left behind by a guest. And by *guest,* she could only assume ex-girlfriend or paramour, given the sheer nature of it.

She shed it and stepped from the shadowed awning. The merciless sun licked at her skin, and she hesitated. As if to give her a reprieve, a fluffy cloud blocked the rays.

Hugo watched her while floating, so only his face was visible, the rest of his body underwater.

"No excuses now," he cajoled.

She hesitated, feet frozen in place. Terror filled her. And yet, it shouldn't. People swam every day. She could stand up at any time, and Hugo was there. Perfectly safe. So, why did her heart beat so fast it almost came out of her chest?

Her mouth was dry, and her steps slow as she neared the edge.

Hugo spoke softly. "Nothing bad will happen."

He sounded surer than she felt.

Her toes curled on the tile of the pool's edge, knowing she stood close enough that if he looked up, he'd be able to tell if she shaved.

Instead, he pushed from the wall and floated on his back, eyes closed. "It's relaxing."

It did look very nice.

She dipped her toe. Not hot, not cold. Taking a breath, she ignored her hammering pulse and sat on the edge and dangled her feet in. She noticed a lack of stairs on either end. No ladder, either. Did he expect everyone who swam to climb out?

Then again, it was his pool.

"You're halfway there."

"Give me a second," she grumbled, staring down and getting her panic under control.

She must have taken too long, because he suddenly surfaced right in front of her, a water beast spraying droplets that made her screech. "Argh!"

"Way to overreact, Ariel. It's just water."

"Which is very wet," she said, lifting her chin.

"No shit." He laughed, which might be why she didn't expect him to suddenly grab her around the waist and drag her into the pool.

He immediately released her, and just as she feared, she hit the surface face-first and floundered. Panicked a second too before her feet touched bottom.

She stood, hair streaming in her face, aware that he was laughing.

"This isn't funny."

"You'd have thought I was killing you. God, I hope the security cameras caught that."

"You're evil!" Through wet hair, she glared at Hugo.

Unrepentant, he grinned. "Don't blame me. You were the one taking too long."

"I was getting in on my own terms."

"You going to be one of those women that whines because I messed up her hair and makeup?" he cajoled.

"I am not wearing makeup." The thin coat of mascara didn't count.

"Then why are you whining?"

"Because you manhandled me."

He waded closer and purred, "Do you know how many women would like to be in your position right now?"

The very idea caused a hot spurt of jealousy. "I am not just any woman."

"You're right, you're not, Ariel, mermaid of the sea and brave explorer."

"I don't know if I'm brave. I was terrified to come in." She had a vague recollection of water making her choke and bobbing for her life like a cork. But only a flash that didn't last.

"You're in now. How do you feel?"

She rolled a shoulder. "Okay, I guess."

"Good, then let's find out if swimming is one of your many skills." He arced off, part porpoise in another life, obviously. He began to undulate in the water, and both his arms rose in a sweeping arc before he plunged.

It looked difficult.

She went more tentatively, the fear of drowning gone, replaced by a worry that she'd look dumb in front of him. Although, why she cared...

She didn't care, but she would admit that he had a point. Perhaps doing what she'd done the night she lost her memory would jog something loose.

In moments, she was swimming too, still clueless about her identity, but finding a certain relaxation in the exercise. She joined Hugo in doing laps—stroke, stroke, breathe, kick, kick, turn. She noticed when she surfaced and swam with her head above the water in a smooth glide that the far end of the pool had a waterfall feature currently undergoing some kind of maintenance. It had tools lying around the base of it, and an electrical cord strung across the patio. Not exactly the safest thing.

The sun returned, beating down viciously, and she cut her swim short. Maybe she'd come back tonight and swim by the light of the stars.

Reaching the edge of the pool, she braced her hands on the side to heave herself only to have Hugo offer a hand.

She glanced up and saw Hugo with a towel slung around his neck.

"Let me help. I don't usually have guests over for swims, so I skipped stairs and ladders for more lap space."

It seemed petty to refuse, and she didn't want to grunt and groan trying to beach herself on the deck. She clasped his hand and squeaked as he pulled her from the water. It happened so fast, she couldn't help but stumble.

Into him.

He caught her, arm sliding around her waist, his body bracing hers, close enough that the hairs on his chest brushed her flesh. Startled, she glanced up at him.

He stared right back. Intent on her. "Slippery when wet."

Wetter than he could imagine. She didn't move away immediately but rather basked in the presence of him. The strength. The virility that oozed from his flesh. She wanted to run her hands down the thick biceps, stroke over his chest and lower.

The sexual tension between them thickened, and his eyes remained open and fixed on hers as his head lowered.

He was going to kiss her. It would be heated and lead to sex. Of that, she was sure. But she couldn't allow it.

She shoved out of his embrace. "Thank you. I

really should get dried off." She almost ran for the stack of towels on a table and ignored his chuckle.

She wrapped one around herself rather than dry off, hiding any revealing flushes of her body. His was now secured around his waist as well, the fluffiness acting as camouflage.

"So, you can swim. What else can you do, little mermaid?"

"I can tell you that your nickname has a patriarchal tone to it that I don't appreciate." Her brow arched.

He laughed. "And we learn even more. Ariel is a feminist."

"I'm glad you find this amusing."

"You're proving to be interesting, especially in what your mind chooses to reveal and not."

"Such as?"

"Let's start with your accent. The way you burr the words indicates a possible southern United States upbringing."

"What accent?" She didn't hear it.

"You don't always unleash it, but when you do, it's unmistakable. I don't suppose you have an urge to call everyone 'sugar?'"

Actually, she bit her tongue on *darling* more often than she was ready to admit. "No, I don't want to call anyone sugar. And just so you know, the name I'd like to use for you isn't that sweet."

He laughed. "I doubt you could call me worse than I've already heard." He flopped into the chair beside hers, the towel still around his waist though doing little to camouflage the rest of his body.

"Let me guess. Arrogant. Brutish. Cad."

"Alphabetically? I am almost tempted to let you keep going just to see what Z would stand for."

"Zany. Because your sense of humor is definitely off-kilter." Her reply came pertly and brought a chuckle to his lips.

"I bow to your excellent grasp of language."

"Stop making fun of me," she grumbled.

"Perhaps your grasp isn't that refined, given that was a compliment."

"I can hear the mockery in your tone when we talk. You still think I'm faking it."

"Honestly, Ariel, I don't know what to think. I'm finding the whole thing rather difficult to grasp."

"You're finding it difficult?" A high-pitched giggle emerged. "I'm the one who got bonked on the head. Who has no recollection of who she is."

"And what would you do if you suddenly recovered those memories?"

"I don't know." She flung out her hands. "But it would be something that didn't involve a rich guy alternating between seduction and baiting."

"You still think I'm trying to seduce you."

She snorted. "Please, no real man wears those kinds of swim shorts."

He glanced down. "They're Speedo. You know, the kind real athletes choose."

"Every woman knows guys who wear them in public do so to show off their junk." Which, admittedly, he had nothing to be ashamed of. Even after being in the water.

His turn to make a scoffing sound. "Your premise is quite inaccurate. I've always worn this type of swimwear because it dries quickly, unlike those shapeless half-pants Americans choose to wear."

"You look ridiculous." A lie but she couldn't back down.

"Would you prefer I remove them?" He arched a brow. "Easily arranged." And then, to her shock, he rose from the chair, hooked his thumbs in the waist, and began to tug.

She turned her head. "You're being juvenile."

"And you're being intentionally mean."

He was right, but that didn't mean she was going to apologize. She glanced back at him. "I'm just trying to clarify that I'm not interested."

"Then that makes two of us. And it also means you won't give a rat's ass if I'm naked in your presence." He began to tug again.

"Don't you dare take those off!"

"I will do whatever I like given this is my property."

The wet bottoms landed in her lap.

"I am not looking!" she growled. "Pervert."

"We'll see who's the pervert."

The implication as she heard him move away

didn't stop Ariel from turning for a peek. The tan lines on his butt followed those ridiculous little shorts. Meaning, he hadn't lied. They were his usual attire.

She stared a moment too long.

A quick glance over his shoulder meant Hugo caught her and winked.

The man was way too sexy. Confident too, which was just as hot in its own way.

Whereas Ariel was a hot mess. She needed another swim.

CHAPTER TEN

HUGO COULDN'T HAVE SAID what possessed him. The woman goaded him, yes, but he was used to being a master at these types of games, which meant that he couldn't explain how it came to be that he strode into his house naked. And worse, got spotted.

Gerome, to his credit, didn't say a word, nor did he look anywhere below Hugo's forehead as he said, "Would you like a robe? I was just bringing one out for you."

"Thank you."

Gerome somehow managed to hand him one without once looking him in the eye. It might have been comical if it weren't pathetic.

Hugo felt as if an explanation might be warranted. "I lost my swim shorts."

"Odd how they can fall off like that."

"I might have given them a hand."

"And can one ask why you felt the need to disrobe in front of our guest?" Gerome ventured, finally meeting Hugo's gaze now that he was covered.

"She made me do it," he grumbled.

"It must have been horrible how she forced you to remove your clothing," Gerome said, quite deadpan.

"She didn't force me. Mostly. But she left me no choice."

"If you say so. Will she agree?"

Hard to tell. "If I promise to apologize, will you stop harassing me?"

"If I were harassing you, you'd know it. But I do agree that an apology is in order for your boorish behavior."

"Later. At dinner."

"Have you invited her?" Gerome asked.

"Er, no. Why would I do that? Doesn't she eat?"

"Given you've been taking meals in your office or out of the house, I've been bringing her trays to wherever she wishes to eat. Today, she had lunch in the garden."

"We'll eat in the dining room tonight."

"What if she says no?"

Hugo blinked at Gerome. "Why would she do that?"

"You did throw your swim shorts at her."

Meaning Gerome had caught part of it. It explained his handy presence with the robe.

"I told you, she made me do it. She dared me," he claimed as if that were all the explanation needed.

In a sense, it was. Male honor demanded that he win.

"I'm sure you misinterpreted her intentions. I've been reading this book," Gerome said, "about the generational gap in expectation that has males acting in a manner most unbecoming for today's enlightenment."

"Did you just roundaboutly imply that I'm a chauvinist? Because I'll have you know, I've taken off my underpants and walked naked before with a bunch of guys I used to run with." A dare combined with alcohol that time.

"For future reference, unless you have permission for coital stimulation—"

"It's called sex. Fucking." Anything but *coital*. That sounded...wrong.

"—the clothes should stay on."

"What if it's a nudist beach or colony?"

Gerome had a placid expression that betrayed nothing.

"I think you should stop reading those new-age, pseudo-psycho books and take your pants off a little more often."

Gerome got even haughtier which, given his demeanor, would have sent most fleeing, thinking he was about to crush them. "I am expanding my mind."

"While I just keep getting dumber. I know. What

can I say? For each gray hair I get, I lose another brain cell." He waved at Gerome. "I am going to my room to get dressed. Remember to invite her to dinner."

"Why don't you do it?"

"Go back out there now while she's mad?" Hugo shook his head. "I'll wait until she's had time to mellow out."

"Maybe she's not too mad. I am pretty sure she was staring at your ass the whole way." Gerome went from giving him shit to encouraging.

She might have been looking, but she'd avoided a kiss. He remembered the way she'd jerked out of his grip. The insult of it might have led to his irrational stripping.

Slashing a hand through the air, Hugo changed his mind. "You know what? Forget dinner. I have plans tonight anyhow." He should keep his distance from the woman who was getting under his skin.

A woman who had him acting entirely out of character. It didn't help that he'd yet to figure out her game. Did she play him? He could usually judge if someone did.

Usually.

However, she proved to be an enigma. A sexy one that had him jerking off in the shower. Not once, but twice. Practically unheard of these days.

At least now, maybe he wouldn't get a boner every time she opened her mouth.

Dressing didn't take long, but he delayed leaving

his room. Maybe he should hunt her down and apologize.

But then apologizing might lead to her smiling at him, and the jesting back and forth might reoccur, and his libido might start taking over his thought process again until he did something even stupider.

Best he leave for the night.

Heading down the hall, phone in hand, he put in a request to have his motorbike brought around.

Gerome met him by the front door with a helmet in hand and a frown on his face. "Where are you going?"

"Out. I have an appointment."

"But dinner..."

"What about it?"

Gerome glanced over his shoulder. "Your guest is waiting for you."

"You invited her to dine?" Hugo's voice rose. "I thought I said not to."

"No, you said you weren't going to do it, so I did it for you," Gerome explained.

"Then undo it."

"I can't just uninvite her. She's expecting you."

"No, she isn't." Ariel suddenly appeared in the parlor entrance, a glass of wine in hand, her red hair loose and flowing around her shoulders, the pale-yellow frock she wore delicate like her features.

"I have an appointment," was Hugo's lame reply.

"Then don't let me keep you. I see you found your pants." Her gaze dropped, and he blushed.

At least, he assumed that's what the heat in his cheeks meant.

"I'll be back late. Don't wait up."

"I wasn't planning to. Have fun with your appointment."

He couldn't have said what made him do it. Why he turned around and said, "Oh, I plan to have plenty of fun, if you know what I mean."

He winked.

Her lips pressed flat.

Hugo sauntered out the front door, knowing that he'd made her jealous and not understanding why it made him so happy.

CHAPTER ELEVEN

THE JEALOUSY TOOK her by surprise. Why would she care what Hugo did and whom with? Let the man take his desires elsewhere. Then maybe he wouldn't be so pathetic in his attempts to seduce her.

Really, tossing his swim shorts at her and strutting off like a stripper with the confidence and the body to pull it off?

In that moment, Ariel really wished she knew whether someone was waiting for her on the other side of this amnesia. Surely, she had someone special in her life. Someone who wouldn't appreciate her flirting and most especially wouldn't like her fornicating with another man.

Because she most definitely liked men.

The door shut, and she heard the purr of a motor-cycle as she headed back to the parlor and the open bottle that she used to refill her wine glass. She twirled the liquid before taking a sip, enjoying the taste, and oddly able to identify parts of the flavor, which she compared to the label. She had a fine palate, apparently.

Gerome followed. "I'm sorry. Earlier, he gave every indication that he'd be joining you for dinner."

"Then changed his mind for a booty call. Can't say as I blame him."

"I assure you, he's not meeting a woman."

"Doesn't matter if he is. Your boss is no one to me other than a host. Which reminds me, I should probably look into moving out given that my memories aren't any closer to coming back."

"Which is exactly why you need to stay," Gerome insisted. "We have the resources here to help you."

"What if I can't be helped?"

"You can't give up yet. It's too soon."

"How did you come to work for Mr. Laurentian?" Ariel asked.

"An old employer of mine died, and Mr. Laurentian, having heard, offered a few of the staff new jobs."

"Kind of him."

Gerome shrugged. "He's a good guy who likes to think he's bad."

"I called him a hero."

"I'm sure that went over well."

Ariel chuckled, recalling the expression on Hugo's face. "You'd have thought I insulted him."

"He's not the type to accept praise."

"Which is odd, given he's quite arrogant."

"You're awfully interested in the boss," Gerome stated.

"Just curious. You have to admit, he poses a fascinating dilemma. Handsome bachelor, who is obviously well-off, lives as a recluse with his faithful everything man."

"He's almost settled down a few times. But things don't always work out."

Gerome said it politely, but Hugo himself alluded to the fact that he'd been burned. Burned badly enough he had no interest in trying anymore.

She felt an odd kinship in that respect. To change subjects, she asked Gerome, "Do you play chess?"

Gerome did, though it turned out she didn't. But, she was sharp at poker.

As the evening waned, she sent Gerome off. The man meant well, but he hovered like a mother hen with a chick. At her age, she should be the mother.

And for a moment, just a second, she saw two faces and briefly got the impression of names: Caroline and Donovan. *My babies.*

Then it was gone again. A brief glimpse that left an ache and a realization. She was a mother, and her children didn't know where she was. Were they worried yet?

Or was she the shitty kind of parent whose progeny avoided them even on holidays? The not knowing gnawed at her.

She took another sip of wine. The third bottle proved as tasty as the first two.

Wandering through the house, barefoot and slightly tipsy, she noted the place had an impersonal feel to it, lacking picture frames or dorky knickknacks with their labels that proved where a person travelled.

It was also too perfect. Obviously, designer-decorated, with each room following a theme. She'd wager that Hugo hadn't selected a single piece in the place. At least the designer he'd hired had a nice style. The kitchen was a modern marvel with a huge gas stove, a massive island, and all the ingredients she needed to bake.

She couldn't have said what prompted it, or how she knew what to grab and how much to measure out. The act of baking seemed as natural as breathing. In no time at all, she had a tray in the oven, and pastries began to take form as she whipped together a custard filling and melted the chocolate for the topping.

By the time she was done, she'd made a dozen fluffy éclairs. She brought one with her to eat in the cozy couch tucked into a window. A place to comfortably watch a chef at work.

She ate the treat and leaned her head back, eyes closed.

What else could she remember without remembering? She could swim. Cook. Argue.

She must have fallen asleep because the next thing

she knew, someone was shaking her and calling her name.

"Ariel! Come on, wake up."

She blinked her eyes and felt sluggish as she slurred, "What's wrong? Why am I outside? Did I sleepwalk?"

"Gas leak in the stove. I got home and found you passed out in the kitchen."

"I guess that explains the queasy stomach and headache." She grimaced. "And it's my fault. I was baking earlier."

"I saw," Hugo remarked, his expression creased in concern. He held her wrist and checked his watch as if counting her pulse. "Are you a pastry chef?"

"I don't know. I don't even know if I'm any good."

"You're really good," Gerome mumbled, striding towards them with an éclair in each hand. "These are delicious." A point reinforced with his bite that squished the filling from the pastry. Not that Gerome wasted any of it. The éclair was gone in two bites.

"Are you sure you should be eating those?" Hugo asked.

"They're fine. But if you're worried, I will take care of the rest," Gerome solemnly promised.

"Don't blame me if you end up sick, then," Hugo grumbled. "I am going to assume by your presence out here that the gas has been shut off. And did you air out the place?"

"Yup."

"I'm sorry I was so careless," Ariel said.

"Wasn't your fault—" Gerome started to say, only to shut up as Hugo gave him a pointed look.

Fuzzy head or not, she understood that there was more going on.

"What is it? Why are you looking at him like that? Is there something you're not telling me?"

"Nothing you need to worry about. I wonder if we should call emergency services to have her checked." Hugo spoke to his butler, not her.

She grimaced. "I'm fine. It was propane gas. It's not like I got carbon monoxide poisoning, or someone lit a match."

"Lucky for us. In that case, if you think you're recovered, let's get you to bed." Hugo scooped her up from the grass, and she pushed against his chest in protest.

"I can walk."

"Just be quiet and let me carry you."

Being cradled in his arms was nice. She gave in and rested her head on his chest. "How was your evening out?"

"A bad idea, apparently, since you can't stay out of trouble."

"You can't seriously blame me for this?"

"You seem to be developing a habit of attracting unfortunate events."

"Not on purpose. Perhaps I am related to the Baudelaire family."

"Who?"

She frowned. "I don't know." The answer slipped from her grasp.

"Where did you get the recipe for those treats?" he asked. "I didn't think we had any cookbooks."

"I baked those pastries from scratch."

"You mean from memory."

"Yes, and yet I couldn't tell you what ingredients or how much right this minute."

"Meaning it's such a familiar thing for you that it's done without even thinking about it.

"Like riding a bike. I guess there are some things you never forget." But why cooking and nothing else?

With what appeared to be effortless ease, Hugo carried Ariel into her room before he set her on her feet. She didn't mean to wobble, but the room suddenly spun.

He grabbed her. "Careful. You're obviously still woozy."

"I'll be okay. Eventually. Maybe." She didn't move out of his grip. Falling down at this point didn't rate high on her list of things to do.

"Let's get you to bed." He helped by pulling back the covers and steadying her as she climbed in.

She lay on her back in the very center of the mattress, and before he could leave, she asked, "Was the gas leak an accident or done on purpose?"

"Doesn't matter."

"Yes, it does," she insisted.

"Then, if you must know, it was an accident. Probably a mouse or something chewed on the line."

She knew he lied. The leak had been intentional.

Rather than let him see her expression that undoubtedly betrayed her feelings, she turned on her side to face away from him. "I seem to be having an uncommonly good run of bad luck."

"I wouldn't say that. Not one of those events has led to you being truly harmed or killed."

"But how long will my luck last?"

CHAPTER TWELVE

UPON LEAVING ARIEL, Hugo's steps grew quicker and quicker as if he could outrun his anger. He only barely contained it as he joined Gerome outside. His man knelt in the bushes behind the kitchen where the gas line fed into the house and the tampering had been done.

Hugo had only seen the lit cigarette by accident, the burning stick of tobacco left behind to light the fuse tied around it, which fed into the house alongside the gas line, which had been tampered with.

Things had almost ended very badly.

"Did you find anything?"

"No. But whoever did this knew what they were doing. The investigators never would have suspected arson. Rather, they would have assumed someone on staff tossed a cigarette too close to the gas and...boom." Gerome exploded his hands, fingers splayed.

"I want every video feed checked. I want to know why nothing was triggered. Where did they come in? Where did they leave? I want a name, Gerome."

"I'll do what I can." Which was usually better than most.

Yet it didn't feel enough for Hugo. He returned to his suite and paced while keeping a digitally trained eye not only on Ariel, who slept restlessly, but also on the patio door to her room, and even the hall outside of it.

They had past coincidence now and headed straight into attempted murder. Someone wanted Ariel gone. Someone who knew that she was staying here.

Or was this related to the hit on him? Could be the pyromaniac didn't realize Hugo had stepped out for the evening. Either way, these attacks had to stop.

The next day, Hugo was loath to leave. With the holes in his security, how could he trust that Ariel would be all right?

He spent the morning in his office mulling over the question of who the explosion had been meant for. He'd not come to an answer when he was interrupted.

A knock on his door preceded Gerome's entrance.

"So?" he said without greeting.

"The cameras that were malfunctioning have been replaced, and I had more added to the circuit."

"How could two cameras go offline without us knowing?" Hugo demanded. He paid for the best.

What happened the night before was unacceptable to him.

Gerome sank into the club chair in front of his desk. "A glitch in the software, at least according to the tech geek I spoke to. The patch for it was somehow never applied."

"Which indicates that someone was aware of the defect in our system and took advantage. Do we have a spy in our midst?"

That would suck given Hugo had personally vetted all the staff. He never would have expected one to betray him.

"If it's a spy, I'd say it's a remote one. I've got Francis working on improving our network's firewall."

"We should have Francis change all the passwords, too," Hugo remarked. "Speaking of whom, I haven't heard from Francis today."

"Because it's Saturday," Gerome reminded. "Most people don't work on the weekends."

"Never understood that," Hugo grumbled. "It's a day of the week like any other."

"Not everyone is as dedicated to their work as you are."

"Are you subtly implying that I have no life?" He arched a brow.

"I wasn't trying to be subtle. Take some time off."

"I've got things that need to be done."

"When are you going to slow down and enjoy life?"

"When are you?" he riposted.

"When your dumb ass does, because who knows what the fuck you'll do if I'm not here to stop you." Gerome stomped off, and Hugo leaned back in his chair.

Yes, he did work a fair bit, but in his defense, the business didn't sleep on the weekends. Or at night. Besides, he had plenty of downtime. He worked from home almost daily now. Which counted as being more relaxed, right?

He tried to concentrate on work in between watching over Ariel, who'd once more chosen to sit by the pool. But this time, she wore a light summer frock. No swimming today.

She seemed recovered from her ordeal the night before. She'd eaten a full breakfast and lunch, according to reports. Gone for a walk in the garden, too.

But he couldn't forget how she'd tossed in her sleep, clearly agitated.

While watching her, an alarm went off—a perimeter sensor that made the watch on his wrist vibrate.

He tapped the warning button that appeared. The screen on the wall went from showing a lovely landscape to being divided into squares, each one representing an active camera feed.

Staff was the cause of the motion in the first few. Ariel once more by the pool, caused the outdoor ones to activate. But he was more interested in the perimeter ones.

"Enlarge the views for the cameras on the northeast quadrant." His house, with its computerized access, obeyed his command and zoomed.

It took him a moment to find the cause of the cameras' alert—new tech he should add. The old set had gone fuzzy. Meaning, there was still a bug in the system, but the ones on the new channel fed him images.

The camouflage the intruders wore did an excellent job of helping them blend in with the foliage Hugo encouraged on the property. Not the best when it came to clear lines for security as Gerome liked to remind him, but Hugo enjoyed the wildness of the greenery.

There was no reason for them to be sneaking onto his property. He spoke into his wristwatch. "Ensure all staff is on high-alert." Some people had Alexa and Google Home systems; Hugo had a custom one with preset commands to use in an emergency.

His wrist buzzed, and he saw a message from Gerome. *Going to intercept.*

Not alone, he wasn't. Hugo planned on helping him. While his staff was well trained on how to act, Hugo wasn't the type to sit back and do nothing while others defended him.

He armed himself first, the holster in his desk taking only seconds to slip on. He headed outside using the door to the garage, then a more subtle exit out of it to the side of his house where the unexpected guests were.

The wild jungle ahead wasn't bright enough to hide Gerome's eye-popping teal shirt. Something patterned in jellyfish, which Hugo silently admired but would never buy.

He flanked his everything man to expand their search net. The mini copse of trees filled a full acre. His oasis when he wanted somewhere *unplugged* to think.

There was serenity to be found walking under the heavy branches, the air immediately more humid, odorous. The hum of insects assailed the senses, as did the rustle of the leaves in the trees.

His watch vibrated. A quick glance showed a simple message.

C U

Gerome, indicating he was aware of Hugo's position. This wouldn't be the first time they'd done something like this together. Gerome had been acting as security pretty much his whole life, although he'd not come to work for Hugo until about twelve years ago.

The first time they'd met, Gerome had been working for another man.

Not a very nice one.

When his employer suffered a freak accident on his boat, Hugo had offered Gerome a position. They'd been together ever since. He counted Gerome among his few friends and trusted him implicitly.

Whoever had infiltrated Hugo's property was good. He almost missed seeing them. Their camouflage gear blended perfectly, and they knew to move slowly. Yet not slow enough. Flickers of motion betrayed them.

Hugo came up behind the person, stealthy as could be. But something must have alerted the intruder to his presence. Just before he could put a gun to the person's head, they whirled and kicked out, the blow to Hugo's hand knocking the pistol free.

His wrist throbbed, but that didn't stop Hugo from grappling with his assailant, his size a little bigger. But that meant little, given his opponent had obviously trained in hand-to-hand.

Every blow Hugo attempted to throw was blocked. He went on the defensive as flying fists and feet came for him, a few landing with bruising impact.

He did his best to dodge and then felt clumsy as he lunged and missed. The intruder's kick sent him reeling, and he hit the ground on his knees.

In sight of his gun.

He grabbed for it and whirled with it in hand, firing on instinct, and then grunting as the intruder slammed into him.

Hugo hit the ground hard under the attacker's weight, and his head banged off a root.

CHAPTER THIRTEEN

THE WATER FELT SOOTHING against flesh determined to be feverish, and not just because of the sun. Ariel had come out to the pool area after lunch in her swimsuit, partially in the hopes that Hugo would join her again.

The man had a way of igniting her senses, especially the spot between her legs. He might not do it on purpose, but the mere fact that he breathed appeared enough to rouse her libido. Dear God, was she a whore in her old life? One who constantly lusted after men?

She frowned and pursed her lips. Why would lusting make her a whore? Weren't women allowed to desire and act upon those desires? The warring opinions on sexuality confused.

She'd take befuddlement over fear. Hugo had lied about the gas leak. It wasn't an accident, meaning yet another attack had been made on her. But why? And by whom? Who wanted her dead?

For some reason, she saw a face, scruffy on the jaw, bloodshot eyes, the mouth twisted in anger.

Tommy. His name is—

Doing another lap, she noticed movement, but not coming from the house. Someone in overalls knelt among the tools by the waterfall.

As Ariel went to touch the wall to do her turn, she got a blurry view of the person, who dangled a cord, the power tool on the end whirring.

Ariel couldn't have said what caused her to launch herself from the water. She hit the deck, and in the same motion, ducked as the other person swung at her, the reciprocating saw narrowly missing.

"What are you doing?" she yelled.

"Killing you, what's it look like?" huffed the attacker as they swung again. Only Ariel wasn't about to be a victim. She ducked and, despite the fear thrumming through her, felt energized and calm.

Perhaps that was why she reached for the assailant rather than running. She grabbed hold and twisted her body, sending the woman into the pool...still holding onto the tool attached to the power cord.

Ariel's mouth rounded in horror as the body in the water jiggled a few times then went still, face-down.

Dead.

Uh-oh.

How would Ariel explain killing her? Would

anyone believe that it was an accident? Not to mention, she obviously wasn't safe here, and whoever wanted her dead was clearly done being subtle.

She eyed the house and ran for it. How long before someone noticed the dead body in the pool? Before they called the police to arrest her?

She wanted to change, a bathing suit wasn't exactly a getaway outfit, but the best she managed was snaring her coverup on the way into the house.

She needed to get away. Now. As far away as she could. She understood the irrationality of it and yet couldn't help herself. Heading out the front door, she winced at the heat of the driveway on her bare feet.

She should have at the least grabbed shoes.

Or a gun. A gun would be nice. She couldn't have said where that thought came from.

Yet the fear wouldn't let her go. She ran parallel to the driveway, the freshly cut grass staining her feet. Then she heard the distant crack of a gun. Or was it?

Her breathing huffed in and out, but she remained focused on the goal. Escape.

Only she never made it past the front gate.

CHAPTER FOURTEEN

HUGO HEAVED the limp body off him, waking with a throbbing head underneath the dead weight. He'd been stunned for a moment when he hit the ground, head wounds were a tricky thing, but other than a soreness to his skull, he discerned no signs of a concussion—no blurry vision, no vomiting, still knew his name and, best of all, he could stand without keeling over.

Gerome tromped through the copse of trees, a body slung over his shoulder. He eyed Hugo for damage. "You okay? You look a little out of it."

"Whacked my head, but fine other than that."

"I'm surprised you got here that fast." Gerome slung the other body to the ground and eyed the one at his feet. The bullet had gone through the chest, probably nicking the heart.

Pity. He would have liked to ask some questions.

By the looks of it, Gerome's target didn't fare any better.

"What are you talking about? I got here the moment I got the alert."

"I take it you didn't have trouble handling the other one, then."

"Wait, there was a third one?" Hugo asked, trying to make sense of Gerome's words.

"Hold on, don't tell me you didn't handle the one sneaking through the back?"

The moment Gerome said it, Hugo flashed on Ariel, by herself and quite possibly a target, too. He sprinted for the rear of the house, heading in the direction of the rear patio, vaulting over a low line of bushes in his way. The fence around the pool required him to grab hold of the rail and climb over. Landing on the other side, he sprinted for the blue waters, his eyes drawn to the body floating on the surface.

Right away, he noticed that it wasn't Ariel. The fully dressed body had short hair and a stockier build. At the bottom of the pool, he saw a power tool with the electrical cord snaking from it.

An accident? An attack? Whatever the cause, that made a third dead body on his property.

And no Ariel.

Where the fuck had she gone? Or had he missed yet another intruder?

Rather than start running around uselessly looking, Hugo bolted for his office and spent a moment flipping through the cameras as he rewound the footage, right past the point where the attack happened. Then he watched. Saw Ariel sluicing her way through the pool, a person wearing utility coveralls and a ball cap pulled low slinking to the cache of tools—a stash that existed because he'd put a halt to the contractor's work given Ariel's presence.

He paused and rewound to the part where Ariel emerged from the water and attacked.

Frame by frame, he saw nothing to indicate that she knew the person was there. As she neared the edge of the pool and the waterfall off to the side of it, she simply slammed her feet down to vault herself. Her hand barely seemed to touch the edge of the pool as she landed on it in a crouch and then sprang.

Ariel caught the assailant's arm and grappled. Not for long, though. She did a move with her hips and then yanked, tossing the attacker into the water—with a live power cord.

Hugo didn't stop the video and thus saw her standing by the edge of the pool, her expression a stricken mask. Horror. Panic. Both emotions and more flashed over her face.

She bolted from the pool area to the house but didn't go to her room. Where had she fled to?

He scrolled through more feeds, room after room. Then the outside. Didn't see her. Scrolled again, assuming he'd missed her on the first pass.

It wasn't until he loaded the front gate footage that

he found her, tugging on the lower bars, then looking up at the sharp points topping them.

Surely, she wouldn't...

She did try and climb. Predictably, she got stuck.

Minutes later, he pulled to a stop beside her on his golf cart and said, "Do you need help getting down?"

She glared at him. "Why is your gate sticky?"

"Because it keeps people from climbing it." He tried to keep his expression deadpan, but she looked comical all twisted in her attempts to extricate herself, which only resulted in her getting even more stuck.

"The stakes at the top weren't enough?"

"Didn't stop you, did it?" he replied. "You know, if you wanted to leave that bad, you could have asked. Gerome or I would have opened it for you."

"I was in a hurry." A bleakness entered her expression.

"On account of the dead body. Understandable."

"It was an accident," she hastily replied.

"If you say so. But it's not me you need to convince."

"You call the police?"

For the moment, he let her think that. "What else was I to do when I found a body floating in the pool, and my guest missing?"

"I didn't mean to."

"Obviously. Which is why I'm guessing you panicked and ran. Where exactly where you going, anyhow? It's a few miles to the nearest trafficked road."

"I don't know. Like you said, I freaked. I didn't have a plan."

"Nothing in your mind except escape." He'd once given in to that impulse, leaving the country of his birth and ending up in the Caribbean.

"Which you foiled. I guess once the cops get here, I'm going to jail."

"Don't be so sure of that."

"Do you mind if we continue this discussion after you get me down? This is massively uncomfortable," she grumbled.

"Say please."

"Please." Hissed through gritted teeth.

He emerged from the golf cart with gloves and the solvent. He'd only recently bought the sticky trap and was pleased to see it worked like a charm. Animals and insects were repelled by the sticky substance, only people seemed to get caught. The stocks he'd bought in that company would be worth a fortune once it went mainstream.

Given she was partway up the fence, he dribbled some solution on the gloves so he could climb up to her without sticking. Then, once he reached her, he sprayed her hands and feet. She'd bolted barefoot with a swimsuit, a coverup, and nothing else.

He couldn't help but mutter. "I've seen dumb things..."

"I panicked, okay."

"You ran off without the slightest clue."

"And failed. Thank you so much for pointing that out."

"Get ready," he said as the solvent loosened the bond between skin and the gate.

She shoved away from the barrier and fell the short distance to the ground where she managed to land on her feet instead of in a heap. That, plus her actions earlier, made him revise his opinion of the woman. She wasn't as defenseless as she appeared.

Yet her expression as she stared at that body... The devastation appeared so real.

She grimaced as she flexed her fingers. "Gross."

Odorous, as well. He peeled off the gloves but could do nothing about the scent clinging to his clothes. "I think we could both use a shower."

"You can do what you like." Her chin tilted. "I'd like to leave. If you would please open the gate."

"We both know I can't do that," he stated firmly.

"If this is about the body in the pool, then it was self-defense."

"I know it was, though that's only part of the reason you can't leave."

"What's the other reason?"

"For one, you need to shower and change."

"I'm fine." She tugged the sheer wrap tighter.

"I can see you're fine. I mean, walking miles barefoot is totally doable." He eyed her feet.

She curled her toes. "I'll grab some shoes and some clothes first before I go."

"Where? I thought you didn't remember anything."

"I don't. But staying here isn't helping. So, I'm going to town. There must be a hostel or shelter where I can spend the night."

"We discussed the fact that they're dangerous. Even if you survive in one, what will you do? Wander around and see if anyone recognizes you?"

"I don't know," she exclaimed. "I guess I'll find a job. I just can't stay here."

"If you're worried about the body, don't be. Gerome will have it handled."

"What's that supposed to mean? I thought you said you called the police."

"I lied."

"Why?"

"Because I am not in the mood to deal with them."

"But the body in the pool—"

"Will be handled. And before you ask, the less you know, the better. If questioned, you were napping this afternoon. You saw nobody."

"You're going to cover for me?"

"Why wouldn't I? Unless it wasn't an accident."

She stared at him. "There is something seriously wrong with you. You should not be this calm about the fact that I killed someone."

"It happens."

"Not in my world, it doesn't," she sputtered.

"How would you know?" he countered slyly.

"Argh," she yelled. "You are impossible."

"Why so upset? We're just talking."

"It's never *just talking* with you."

"What else would it be? My lips are moving. Sound is coming out."

"You do it on purpose to drive me nuts."

"If you're getting offended, then that is your own fault."

She pursed her lips. "Just who are you?"

"Hugo Laurentian."

"*What* are you?"

His lips quirked. "Not a very nice man."

For some reason, that caused her to frown. "Why would you say that?"

"You're the only one who has ever called me a hero. Most choose less flattering terms."

"And do they have a reason to dislike you?"

"Most definitely." Hugo wasn't one to back down when things got ugly. Especially since he was usually the one causing the ugly.

"All the more reason for me to leave."

"Or to stay. After all, if I am a dangerous man, then perhaps leaving would be worse. You know my secrets now."

"What secrets?"

"You tell me."

"Not the spy thing again," she huffed. "I haven't been anywhere near your office."

She hadn't, and yet...something about her triggered a sense of warning. Caution. "Would you like to see my office?"

"No."

"Are you sure? I have a very nice desk. Big and sturdy." He intentionally baited her, and she fell into the trap.

She waggled a finger at him. "That's enough. I'm on to the innuendos. I see what you're doing, and you will stop."

"And just what am I doing?"

"Flirting with me so I'll sleep with you. I'm telling you right now, it won't happen."

"And you got all that from me offering to show you my office? Don't flatter yourself, Ariel." But he had been teasing mostly to gauge her reaction. Hot and hotter. Even now, as she argued against her attraction, he could see the flush of her skin.

"I might be married," she declared.

A claim that discomfited. "Would that stop you?"

Rather than reply too quickly, she took a moment, her brow knitted as if she concentrated. "I'm going to say it would. I don't think I'm a woman who would cheat on someone."

"That would be a rarity," he mumbled as he swung back into the driver seat of the cart he'd driven over in.

"You had someone betray you?" She stood alongside him.

"More than once. Meaning, I'm sure the problem lies with me." He didn't think he asked for much of his partners. Discretion. Loyalty in and out of bed. That they have some semblance of fondness for him. But at the same time, he wanted them to have a mind of their own. He hated *yes* people. A true partner wouldn't be afraid to argue.

"No one should ever be cheated on," Ariel hotly declared. "It's the ultimate betrayal."

"I would agree." He also counted his blessings that in the case of one of those cheats, he'd found out before the wedding. Janet had fooled him thoroughly. "And to put your mind at ease, I will reiterate my promise to not lay a hand on you. You shall be the one to decide if and when it happens."

"Never."

He almost laughed at the too-vehement reply. "Never say, never, Ariel."

"I'm not a floozy." She tossed her hair.

"Nothing wrong with knowing what you want and taking it. Sexuality isn't a crime."

"But cheating on a partner is."

"Then it's a good thing you've not done anything that would break any vows." Not yet, at least. "Come back to the house," he said, gesturing to the seat in the golf cart beside him. "We'll figure shit out, and if you still want to leave, I'll make sure you have money and a place to go."

She shook her head. "I can't take your charity."

"Why not?"

"Because it wouldn't be right. Not to mention, I shouldn't involve you. Obviously, there's something wrong with me. Why else would someone attack me?"

Hugo could have mentioned the possibility that the person had been sent to kill him, but instead, he said, "The good news is, that person is now gone."

Her lips turned down. "Because I killed them."

"Better them than you."

"True." She sighed and finally flopped onto the seat beside him. "Despite what you think, I should come clean with the police. It will be better if I'm honest now rather than later when they uncover the truth."

"What makes you think I won't just get rid of the body?" The thought had crossed his mind.

"Did you?"

"No." Because all it took was an accomplice who'd videoed any of the action, or for a traitor in his midst to reveal what had happened. "But don't worry, Gerome will have arranged the scene by now and ensured that you aren't implicated."

"Who are you?" she asked again suddenly. "And don't feed me a line about being a businessman."

"So, you want me to lie?"

"Business guys don't even think of staging a murder scene for the cops."

"Don't be so sure. Let me ask, do you really want to try telling Pierrot the truth? What would that accomplish?"

"Maybe the police could help find out why that person came after me."

"Because they've shown themselves to be so adequate thus far."

Her lips pursed. "Good point. But here's the problem, what if I lie and they find out?"

"They won't," he assured.

She eyed him. "This doesn't make sense. Two days ago, you accused me of trying to get close to blackmail you somehow. Now, you're helping me hide the fact that I murdered someone."

"Hard for you to blackmail me when I have evidence that could put you in jail."

Her eyes rounded, but rather than lambast him, she laughed. A deep, throaty sound. "Well, I'll be damned. That's actually brilliant."

"I know." He spun them around and trundled the cart back to the house. "A few things to ensure we pull this off. Before you shower, put your suit and wrap outside the door. We'll have them cleaned so there's no evidence you were near that pool or the body. And remember your cover story."

"Napping all afternoon. Saw nothing." She heaved out a deep breath. "I don't know why you're so calm about this or helping. But, thank you."

"Thank me after we've gotten rid of Pierrot." A feat that would likely require him to sponsor a new car for the fleet.

CHAPTER FIFTEEN

THE GOLF CART stopped by the house where they separated. She quickly made her way to her room, encountering no one on the jaunt. The staff was discreet, and there were fewer about than expected. But despite the lack of real eyes, she was conscious of the electronic ones tracking her. All providing more evidence of her crime.

It discomfited to know that Hugo basically owned her. That he could demand anything of her in return for his silence.

I should ask Tanya to wipe his security footage.

She blinked. Who was Tanya? The knowledge of the name slipped through her grasp.

The door to her room slammed shut behind her as her irritation manifested. She hated these glimpses because they only served to highlight just how much she'd forgotten.

She quickly stripped, leaving her sticky garments outside the door, doing it discreetly lest anyone see her naked body. She didn't dare use a clean towel just in case she left some residue. Because who the heck turned their gate into some kind of giant-sized fly trap?

The shower and some soap removed the gross film on her skin. The hot water soothed some of her tension, but it couldn't erase what she'd done.

She'd killed someone. The horror of it remained, but so did her analysis of the situation, which clearly indicated that she had no choice. That person in the utility coveralls had attacked her. It was kill or be killed. If she had to, she could plead self-defense.

If it came to that.

Hugo claimed that it would look like an accident that wouldn't involve her at all. Could she trust him? She didn't understand his motive in helping her. Not with covering up the death, or the fact that he brought her to his house in the first place.

If his plan was seduction, then shouldn't he have tried harder by now? Perhaps he enjoyed stringing her along. Or maybe she read the situation wrong, and he wasn't attracted to her at all.

The summer frock she chose had a sweet innocence to it with its frilly white edging and pastel floral pattern. She left her hair loose and soft with a slight wave from only blow-drying it partially and then letting it air-dry.

A knock at the door wasn't unexpected, yet she let

out a squeak. A little high-strung. She should have indulged in a glass of wine to relax.

The sharp rap came again. "Ariel, it's Gerome."

Indeed, opening the door showed Gerome hulking in the hall.

What did one say to the man who'd just covered up a crime scene for her? "Hi."

"Hey. I heard what happened. You okay?" The man's concern appeared sincere.

She nodded. Physically, yes. Mentally, she was a hot mess.

"Everything is going to be fine. Boss will make sure of it."

"Your boss must be remarkably well-connected if he can guarantee that."

"He'll do right by you."

"Hopefully, he doesn't have to do anything at all."

"Guess we'll see. The superintendent wants to see you," Gerome stated.

"Of course, he does. How come he's always the one to investigate? Shouldn't he have like underlings handling stuff?" she asked as she joined Gerome in the corridor.

"Pierrot could and should, but he takes a special interest in the boss."

"Because of the money."

"More because the police force is understaffed, overworked, and underpaid. While the boss might grumble, he doesn't actually mind helping out. A safe island with a low crime rate is better for everyone."

She paused in the hall and whispered, "Did he believe it?" She didn't elucidate on the *it* part.

"Why wouldn't he?" Gerome said easily. "Poor maintenance worker must have gotten tangled in the cord and fallen in. I was horrified when I found the body. The boss immediately called for help while I turned off the power. Alas, we couldn't resuscitate."

She blinked at him. "Wow. That is actually a believable scenario."

"Because that's what happened. You saw nothing," Gerome reminded. He put a finger to his lips and continued on his way, leading her into the mysterious office she'd yet to see. Upon entering, her gaze immediately went to Hugo, who stood at a window rather than behind the massive desk. The wood was some striated light and dark masterpiece that probably cost more than she'd like to imagine. The chair behind it was lush and leather-covered.

From more leather club seats facing the desk, the superintendent stood and sketched a partial bow. "Mademoiselle, a pleasure to see you despite the wretched circumstances."

"I just heard. How utterly awful." She hoped she didn't overdo the wide-eyed shock. "To think I swam in that pool just yesterday."

The notepad emerged. "Were you by the pool today?"

She nodded. "For a while, just after lunch. Then it got too hot, and my head started to hurt, so I went to my room."

"Do you recall seeing anyone?"

She shook her head. "No. Sorry. First I heard of it was when Gerome fetched me and said you wanted to talk."

"You showered," Pierrot remarked.

"Who can help but shower a few times a day in this humidity?" She wrinkled her nose and fanned herself.

"Better than the rains," Jacques declared. "Would you mind looking at some pictures of the victim?"

Hugo's tone was sharp as he said, "She already told you she didn't see anyone."

"Maybe not today. But could be she recognizes them because the person we fished from your pool does not work for the maintenance company."

"You mean someone came here on false pretenses?"

Did Pierrot hear the mocking tone in Hugo's voice?

Ariel hastened to intervene. "I'd be glad to look at pictures. Anything to help."

"You might want to sit. They are a little shocking." Pierrot indicated the seat alongside his, bringing her close, and then he moved in closer still to angle his phone.

"Showing her dead bodies? Really?" Hugo snapped.

132

"It's okay. I'm sure I can handle it." She took a deep breath to steady her nerves.

"Ready?" Pierrot held out his phone. "Just tell me if you recognize them."

She briefly eyed the splayed figure on the screen, the overalls shapeless and neutral in appearance. The face that of a stranger.

She shook her head. "Nope."

"Are you sure?" Jacques swiped and offered her a close-up of the face, the features forever frozen because of what she'd done.

A violent recoil saw Hugo heading for her and barking, "Enough. Can't you see you're upsetting her?"

"My deepest apologies," the police chief said, a statement lacking sincerity despite the deprecating expression on his face.

"I'll be fine." She let Hugo place his hand on her shoulder. She needed some steadying.

"One has to wonder why a person who wasn't an actual maintenance worker would go to the trouble to trespass and somehow fall into the pool."

"It is not my job to wonder why criminals do what they do. It is yours," Hugo replied.

"And part of that job is deciphering motive. What possible reason could they have for being here?"

A sneer pulled Hugo's lips. "Look around. Pretty obvious, I'd say."

Before things got ugly, Ariel stood and wrung her hands. "This entire thing is just highly upsetting. First, someone tries to kill me at the hospital, then a burglar dies in the yard of the house where I'm staying. I don't feel safe at all." She laid it on a bit thick, but Jacques acted as if stung.

In a sense, he was. "We do an excellent job staying on top of crime. Perhaps the problem is your remote location. Given the new circumstances, I'd like to reiterate my offer for accommodations."

Hugo wasn't about to let her agree. "There's no reason for her to leave. It was merely an unfortunate accident."

"A lot of those lately, it seems," Jacques stated, tucking away his notepad.

"Too many," she agreed. "Which is why I would never dare accept your offer and inflict the troubles plaguing me on you. I need you at your best to do your job and find out who I am." She smiled to take the sting out of the rebuke.

The superintendent still bristled. "In that case, I shall leave you so I may go and continue my investigation. If you remember anything, though..."

"Actually," Hugo said, holding up his hand.

"Yes?" The police chief eyed him with sudden suspicion.

"This is more of a favor than a clue. It turns out, I bought a car that I have no use for. I don't suppose you could use another patrol car?"

"You are too kind." The rest of their conversation faded as Hugo escorted Jacques out, leaving Ariel to pace the office. The walls were barren of bookcases. Just painted a cream color with vivid artwork on two of them. Thick floor-length drapes lined the patio door. The desk provided a focal point with only two chairs facing it. Stark and yet expensive. The room could have used some kind of ornate yet masculine sideboard. How could she gauge these things at a time like this?

What else could she do but admire the stonework on the floor, the pattern intricate and expertly laid?

Hugo slipped back into the office a moment later. "He's gone."

"For now. Possibly not for long. I don't think he bought it."

"I think he's got his doubts, but I know Pierrot. He'll hint at something else needed for the station before he outright accuses me of anything."

"What do you mean, *you*? I'm the culprit."

"He likes you. He'll blame me first."

"If that happens, then I will tell the truth."

Hugo shrugged. "If it makes you feel better. I doubt you'll go to jail. More likely, he'll have a proposition for you, too."

She cast him a glance. "He can propose, it doesn't mean I'll accept."

"We all do things in our life we're not proud of in order to survive." A cryptic thing to say. He grabbed some glasses from the tray on his desk but left the decanter alone. "I think we need a drink."

"Make it a double. It's been a hell of a day."

"It could have been worse."

"Worse how?" she asked. "Someone died."

"But *we* didn't."

"That's not exactly reassuring."

"I don't bullshit."

She expelled a heavy breath. "Well, maybe you should try. You might be acting all cool and blasé about having a dead body in your pool, but I'm a mess. A part of me feels like I should be in more shock, that I should feel more guilt, maybe run after the police chief and confess."

"That would not be useful."

"See, and it's statements like that which make me wonder if I should be listening to you. Are you a crime lord of some kind?" It would explain the wealth.

"What if I said '*yes*?'"

She blinked at the unexpected reply. "Are you really?"

"It's complicated. But suffice it to say, I do things the law wouldn't approve of."

"Like hide the truth. Now that you've told me that, does this mean you're going to kill me so I can't tell anyone about you or anything I've seen?"

"I would never kill you."

She almost sighed in relief until he added, "I'd hire someone, of course."

She glared at him, and he had the temerity to laugh.

"Lighten up, Ariel. While I might not be a good guy, I'm also not a murdering psychopath."

"Why couldn't you pretend to be some kind of philanthropist who gives to the poor? It's a more attractive look."

"I thought women loved bad boys."

For a moment, a face flashed in front of her mind's eye, the sneer on it, and the look in the eyes a match for the dark hair flopping over a brow creased in anger. "Not all women." The image faded, and she spaced out a minute before tuning back in.

"...out tonight."

"What?"

"I said, with everything that's happened, we need a night out."

"I'd say that's the last thing I need."

"What else are you going to do? Sit in your room and watch television?"

"I was going to have wine and maybe some cheese." Because, personally, she thought barricading herself in her room with a weapon sounded smarter than going out.

"You'll never learn anything by staying inside."

"What if I'm recognized?"

"Isn't that the point?"

"By the wrong person," she snapped. "Or have you forgotten, I was attacked?"

"By a burglar."

"Or a hired killer." She flung out her hands. "I have a target on my back."

"Maybe they meant to kill me."

She snorted. "Really? Is that what you're going with?"

The grin he wore was much too handsome. "A man wants to feel important."

"I wish they were trying to kill you," she muttered.

"Guess we'll never find out for sure who their target was. Maybe next time, you'll leave them alive so we can question them."

Her anger faded as quickly as it came. "It really was an accident."

"I know. Which is another reason for you to come out with me. You need to get your mind off things."

"I can't eat."

"Then ignore the food, but there will be alcohol. And possibly some nudity."

She arched a brow. "Mine, or yours?"

"The entertainment. I am supposed to attend a private party."

"Is it really the right time to be going to one?"

"Never better if we want to throw Pierrot off the scent. Since you shouldn't be alone, you're coming with me."

"I'm really not in the mood."

"Too bad. You're accompanying me, and that's final."

The command straightened her spine. "Don't you

dare pull the patriarchal nonsense with me, sugar. I will make my own decisions, starting with the one where I stay here."

"Then I'll stay with you. We'll change into some comfy clothes, get some buttered popcorn, throw on a movie in the parlor. Maybe even get a fire going. Do you like wine?"

The intimacy he suggested caused even more panic to run through her than the thought of leaving the house with him. A few glasses of wine, and she might forget her resolve to keep her hands off him. Might not care that, on the other side of her memory wall, someone might be waiting for her.

"On second thought, you're right. A change of scenery sounds perfect. After all, what can anyone do to me while we're in public?"

He leaned close. "More than you'd think if there's a tablecloth." And with that outrageous statement, he walked away. She changed her panties before they left.

INTERLUDE: BACHELORETTE PARTY

A FLASH of red hair caught Carla's eye, the shade very familiar. She turned to see Meredith stepping into the club wearing a cute floral-pattern summer dress. Not her usual slinky attire. She had her hair drawn back, her makeup almost nonexistent, and if it weren't for the fact that they knew each other so well, Carla might have thought her friend had a doppelganger.

She clung to the arm of some stranger, a big man, wearing a suit in a place that usually showed more skin, not less. The floor they were on, the ground-level, acted as a lounge with comfortable chairs and loveseats scattered about with tables to set drinks. A haze of smoke filled the air, clinging to skin and clothes, coating the lungs. As an ex-smoker, she couldn't stand the smell of it anymore and missed the laws governing her state.

Serving the patrons were waiters, male and female

wearing black bottoms and white tops, but that was as far as the uniform aspect went. Some chose booty shorts and tied-off blouses. Others went with actual slacks and collared shirts.

Those working the floor grabbed drinks from the bartender, who also served a long, curving bar, the surface of it gleaming in the neon lights that ran along its edge. It was the brightest thing in the room with the rest of the dim lighting. Despite seeing lips moving all over, Carla couldn't really catch more than a few words here and there as the thumping of the music upstairs blended with the hum of conversation.

When the song paused, she could hear a roar, dancers waiting for the next beat. The second floor was the lively section with dancing and live shows. Guess where the bachelorette party was scheduled to happen?

She already wore her crown that said *bride*. Wore the silly clipped-on veil. But the rest of her was anything but virginal, although she'd chosen to wear white. The skin-tight dress was a splurge—on Meredith's urging as a matter of fact.

She'd taken Carla shopping and made her buy the form-fitting thing. It was worth the price tag when she saw Philip's face as she blew him a kiss before getting in the blacked-out Suburban that'd brought them to the club.

He was off to his bachelor party, despite his

protests that he'd rather not. He'd watched the movie, *The Hangover* with her and elucidated all the very valid reasons men should never have one last hurrah.

She'd kissed him and said words that still held power for her, "I trust you." Loved and trusted Philip in a way she'd never expected to experience. She just didn't trust others to keep their hands off her man.

Carla stood on tiptoe and made a point of moving enough to draw the eye. Meredith never once roved her gaze around. Not even to check out the room.

First odd thing.

Second? Meredith kept herself tucked, shoulders a bit rounded, a look Carla had never seen before. Was Meredith okay?

The sharp whistle Carla blew had a bunch of people looking around, but there was only one she intended it for. Meredith's gaze danced around the place, even briefly alighting on Carla. Then it moved on without even a hint of acknowledgement.

The urge to barge over and force a conversation occurred to Carla. She was very proud of her self-control, especially since Mother had told them she was on a mission. A mission that didn't require backup?

Meredith and the man entered a door at the far end of the place, the one leading to the private lounge. Fuck being discreet. Carla was going in for a peek.

Before Carla could march into that private party, though, Tanya noticed her lagging and waylaid her. "Where are you going? The party is upstairs."

Tanya had her blond hair in two ponytails, one on each side, both streaked pink. She'd gone for a bright look this evening, something she did more often now. It suited her.

"I just saw Merry going in there with some guy." She angled her head, knowing Tanya would figure it out.

"You didn't know him?"

Carla shook her head. Before she could reply, the rest of her wedding party returned and surrounded her.

"What's wrong?" Audrey asked. She looked soft and sweet in a romper that ended at mid-thigh. It did an excellent job of hiding the shape of the pistol she had strapped to the inside of her leg.

"Merry's acting weird."

"You saw her?"

"I did, too," Portia stated. "She and some guy were getting out of a sports car when I got here."

"I saw it. Porsche. A sweet ride." Louisa whistled. "My Rosy has always wanted one of those."

"No surprise that Merry found herself a rich one to play with. Think he'll last until the wedding?"

"Three days? I think it depends whether he tries to pin her down. He mentions serious and long-term, and she is gone." Tanya waved a hand and almost took out a tray of drinks precariously balanced as the waiter passed.

"One day, she's going to find the right one," Audrey

143

stated. "Like we did." The tight group had finally shed their pasts and, in some cases, their roles with the agency that gave them a second chance. Carla had more or less left the agency but did the occasional mission for fun. Tanya was doing hacking only these days and working with her new live-in boyfriend.

Audrey had told her just that morning that she was pregnant. She and Mason couldn't be any happier.

As for Carla, she was getting married.

She needed tequila and something to work off the stress. She glanced upstairs. Dancing would help.

"Hey, who wants to see what he looks like?" Louisa asked. "I've got video."

"How did you get footage before me?" Tanya exclaimed. She was usually the one burrowing into the networks.

"Rosy is in there and saw them coming in. She's never met Merry and asked me who the hot redhead was."

"I want to know who the hunk is," Audrey said. Upon peeking at Louisa's phone, she whistled. "I can see why Meredith ditched us. That man is all kinds of handsome."

"Don't let Mason hear you say that, or he's bound to spank you," teased Tanya, a change from the mom who'd previously turned red at the mention of sex.

"I should be so lucky." Audrey fanned herself. "Ever since he found out I was pregnant, he's been super overprotective and is talking about us getting a house in suburbia."

"The horror!" someone said, and the group laughed.

Carla, however, wasn't amused. She pointed to Merry on the screen. "Mission or not, three days before my wedding, and she acted as if she didn't know me," Carla complained. She missed the reassuring presence of the older woman.

"If she's working, then she obviously doesn't want to blow her cover." Portia took her side, but only briefly as Tiger Mom, living up to her name, checked in on her twins via the remote camera she'd set up.

Again.

Carla elbowed her. "They're fine. Aunt Judy is not going to let anything happen to them." The Aunts were retired agents who acted as security for the moms' families when they had to go on missions.

"She is letting them watch television." A frown marred Portia's features.

"Let the kids live a little. They're on vacation." Carla rolled her eyes.

"She has a point. They'll be okay," Tanya jumped in to reassure.

"Television rots the brain. My girls are only allowed three hours a week watching preapproved documentaries. No video games. No social media," Portia said with pride.

"Which explains why they're weird," Carla muttered.

Portia glared.

Tanya tried to defuse the situation. "We should ask Mother about Merry and her beau before we barge in. Where is she?"

It was Carla who noticed the woman with dark skin in a bold, red dress, her crimped hair bobbing, au natural and glorious.

"Doesn't look like Mother is planning to join us."

The ones with their backs to Mother couldn't turn to look, not without drawing attention, but Louisa whistled. "Your mom is looking hot tonight."

Tanya wrinkled her nose. "Don't talk like that about Mother."

Mother swung her hips and didn't look at them once as she entered the private lounge in the back via the same door Meredith had used.

It was Audrey who said, "Looks like they're ditching us for the bachelor party."

The men weren't into the same kind of dancing as they were. Having met Percy, the pranking best friend Philip had from his military days, there would be some naked women.

She thought of Philip. And naked women.

"Ladies, change in plans. What do you say we crash the bachelor party a little earlier than planned?"

It was Tanya who snared the waitress as she passed

with her tray of shooters. "To the bride!" She held up the glass.

"To the bride!" they said before tossing them back. With liquor warming their bellies, they plotted their ambush.

CHAPTER SEVENTEEN

THE MOMENT ARIEL stepped onto the pavement outside the club, she wanted to go home.

Except she didn't have a home, just Hugo's house. Beautiful, luxurious but also very temporary. She had nowhere to go. No one to protect her.

The reminder got her inside, where the number of people had her huddling close to Hugo.

He placed his hand over hers. "No one will do anything here. It's too public."

It should have reassured, and yet she found herself anxious. Would someone in here recognize her? What if no one did?

The fear of either scenario kept her head tucked and her body close to Hugo's as he navigated them through the room to the far side of the club. Awareness prickled her skin, a crawling feeling. Was she watched?

A sharp whistle drew her awareness, and she

glanced over to see a room full of people not paying her any attention, except for a woman in a spectacular white dress.

Her intent look pinned her, and Ariel couldn't hold the gaze. She glanced away. Why did that woman stare? Was it jealousy? Did she know Hugo?

The very idea that he might have been with that beautiful woman irritated. It shouldn't have, but it did.

She kept expecting the staring woman to confront them. Perhaps start a row with Hugo in public. Instead, they stepped from the buzzing bar area and entered a quieter, private lounge. She couldn't help but glance over her shoulder, wondering if the woman would follow.

The door swung shut, blocking her view. Her actions didn't go unnoticed.

"Something wrong?" Hugo asked.

"Nothing." She bit her lower lip and explained, "Or maybe something. There was a woman staring at me. Us."

He immediately halted. "Why didn't you say so? Maybe she knows you." He began to pivot, but she stopped him, the hand she had looped with his arm urging him to remain.

"I didn't recognize her."

"Maybe if you got close."

She shook her head. "I don't think it will make a difference. Could be she was looking at you."

"Me? Why?"

Was he truly that dense, or fishing for a compliment? "You're handsome and rich. I'm surprised we haven't been mobbed."

"I don't go out often. No one knows me well outside of my villa. So, I doubt the woman was looking at me. Let's go see."

When he would have moved, Ariel pulled free. "We can't go back out there."

"Why not?"

"Because what if I'm wrong and she wasn't looking at all?"

"Then no harm."

"I don't want to," she huffed, in a bit of a panic.

"What if she knew you? What if meeting her jogs your memory?" Hugo asked.

"What if I find her and it turns out I still don't remember? Every time I turn a corner or come across a new face, I have this hope that everything will suddenly return to me. Each time, I'm disappointed." She ducked her head. "What if I am nobody forever?"

"First off,"—his hand cupped her chin to bring her gaze up to meet his—"you are not nobody. You are Princess Ariel, survivor of the sea and snake, vanquisher of the fake repair person."

She wrinkled her nose. "I could have done without the reminder."

"It's to show you that you are a fighter. You keep persevering."

"I am muddling along, trying to figure out who I

am. And failing. The person you just described isn't real."

"You feel real to me."

She glanced at his face. He had his entire focus on her. It pleased and discomfited at once. What did he see when he looked at her? Because when Ariel looked in a mirror, she barely recognized the face. How had she gotten the scar on her belly? What of the one on her arm?

"What if I don't like myself?" she admitted.

Hugo could have said many supportive things at that point, but he said the one thing that had her squaring her shoulders instead. "Don't be a coward. If it turns out you don't, then fix it. You don't give up."

Her chin lifted. "You're right." Why was she waiting for a revelation to find *her*? She was strong. She could do this.

Ariel strutted back out into the main bar area, her gaze tracking the room, looking for the woman who'd stared at her. One thing nagged her.

If they were acquainted, and Ariel had been missing, surely a friend of hers would have rushed over to check on her welfare.

The woman was gone, and she felt foolish. "Sorry," she mumbled.

Hugo squeezed the fingers she had on his biceps with his free hand. "Don't stress about it."

"Easy for you to say."

"It is. But I am sure you can worry enough for the

both of us." He was non-apologetic as he walked them back into the private lounge filled with eight men and two women, one of them a waitress in black and white, bringing them drinks.

At least she wouldn't be the only female at the party. Gang-bangs were only fun in the movies. In real life, chafing started at number three.

She blinked.

Ariel didn't want to know how or why she remembered something like that.

The other female sat in the back, phone in hand, not paying the room any attention. She had her blond hair shaved on the sides and back, but long on top. Her tight shirt showed off an enviously sized bosom and ample cleavage.

A man rose from a table and waved. "Hugo." The guys strode for each other in the manner those who are old friends do. There was some back-slapping and a handshake. Then an enthusiastic back and forth about how things had been and comments on Hugo's luck in living in paradise.

She tilted her head and looked at the man. The name came to her tongue a mere second before Hugo said it.

"Ariel, I'd like you to meet an old acquaintance of mine, Mason. Mason, this is Ariel."

She liked that he didn't mention the fact that Ariel wasn't her real name. She held out her hand, and

Mason hesitated only a beat, barely a second, and yet she noticed it.

"Ariel, is it? Lovely to meet you."

"Have we met before?" she asked boldly. "You seem familiar."

Brow creased, Mason glanced at Hugo instead of her, as if asking for permission to speak.

It was at that moment that they were interrupted.

A woman with smooth, dark skin grabbed Mason's arm. "There you are. I need to speak with you. About your fiancée." A heavy French accent rolled the consonants.

"Hey, Marie. Is everything all right with Audrey?"

"She's fine. But you need to come chat with me. It's been too long, *mon petit chou*."

Mason shrugged as he was dragged off.

Whereas, Hugo frowned. "I wonder who that woman is. I don't believe I've ever met her before."

Given that Marie was gorgeous, Ariel could see why he would be interested. It didn't make her words any less tart. "Then maybe you should go after her," she snapped.

He glanced at her. "Why?"

And that quickly, her jealousy evaporated. She was acting crazy. "That man. Who is he?"

"Mason. Who I might add is practically married with a kid."

"I thought he acted oddly."

"Did he?"

She frowned. "As if he knew me but pretended not to. Why would he do that?"

"The only reason I can think of has you as ex-lovers." That brought a scowl to his lips. "That would be unfortunate."

"Meaning?"

He glanced down at her. "Nothing. Shall we tour the room and see if anything else jogs your memory?"

"I'd rather leave. You do realize there's hardly any women here."

"Give it a few more minutes. The entertainment is about to start." He angled for the stage.

She understood the implication. "You brought me to a strip show?" she hissed. She wasn't sure if she was outraged or titillated.

"They don't just strip. They dance, too. But don't worry, they'll mostly be harassing, Philip, the groom-to-be."

"You brought me to a bachelor party?" She couldn't help the incredulous tone.

He smiled. "I did."

She could have freaked out more, but then she remembered what he'd said about choosing how she wanted to be. The type of woman who hid and whined from the world, or the kind that boldly prepared to watch women strut their stuff on a stage. With her hand on his arm, and her head held high, she found it easier than expected to mingle as Hugo said "hello" to a few more people in the room. Including some guy called Devon who was dating the bride's best friend. From the sounds of it, she had a few close gal pals who'd all come for the destination event.

It made Ariel wonder if she had a circle of close female friends. Or did she have a cat? What if she owned a bunch of them and because she was missing, they starved?

"What's wrong?" Hugo asked. "You got this holy-shit look on your face."

"Do I look like a cat lady to you?"

"Nah."

She sighed.

"Maybe dogs, but more like goats. I'll bet you raise those little goats that are so popular these days and dress them in pajamas." He said it quite seriously.

"Not funny."

"Only because you fear it might be true."

He deserved the glare.

The lights flickered and dimmed, the show about to start. He led her to a table off to the side at the back. She appreciated the discrete location but liked, even more, the glasses of wine he ensured kept coming. He had his back to the stage, not even turning his head when the music started.

A dancer strutted out, her white dress skin-tight and showcasing a lovely figure. She wore a mask over her tanned features and a fluffy boa around her neck.

Marie stood from her table and began moving for the stage. Perhaps she wanted a closer peek.

The woman on the stage looked right out over the front rows, and Ariel could have sworn she sought her out. In that moment, she knew it was the same woman she'd seen earlier, the one who'd been staring at her.

Back again now. Staring once more. Her fingers moved intricately in a pattern that felt familiar. Some kind of dance move, maybe? She almost wanted to reply but kept her hands tucked in her lap.

Movement at the back of the stage drew her eye to a face peeking from the curtains, the shape of the nose, the lips, the hair...

Audrey.

The name came and stayed. But no other context with it. And probably a guess, given Ariel had heard that guy Mason mention it earlier.

The woman on stage was joined by another and another, which seemed confusing until she realized they all had significant others in the crowd. The dancers, who never stripped, were helped off the stage, and much laughter arose as they all began to mingle with the men.

Hugo smirked. "Happens every single time."

"You expected the party to get crashed."

"It's become a bit of a tradition."

"Who are the bride and groom?" she asked.

"The one wearing the crown in that guy's lap."

"Duh," she exclaimed. "I meant names."

He leaned closer. "Are you sure you don't know?"

She scanned the couple again. "They don't even seem vaguely familiar."

"I don't know the bride myself. I'm an old friend of her grandfather's and the groom."

Her gaze kept darting from face to face, and it didn't help that she kept seeing them staring right back. But none approached.

None of them knew her. She imagined things.

It became too much. She rose. "I need to leave. My head hurts." She didn't wait for a reply but fled, and only as she reached the sidewalk outside, did she notice that Hugo had followed.

He tucked her hand back on his arm. "It will be a minute before the car comes around."

"I'm sorry. You shouldn't leave the party. I'll be fine."

"I'm not big on parties, and I think you need me more right now. You remembered something."

She wrinkled her brow. "No, not really, but I swear all those people were watching me. It's probably me being paranoid, but it was driving me nuts."

A woman stepped outside, the one in the white dress. The bride. "Hey, you guys all right?" she asked, but her gaze was on Ariel.

"Fine." Ariel faked a smile. "Congrats on the wedding. When's the big day?"

"Tomorrow," the woman said, still eyeing her.

"I am sure it will be beautiful." The valet brought

the car, and she practically leaped into it. Anything to avoid the woman's dark gaze.

It made her head throb even harder.

Hugo joined her, sliding into the driver seat, but waited until they pulled away to say, "I don't think you're crazy anymore."

"I never knew you did," she grumbled.

"That woman was eyeballing you something fierce."

"Right? But if she knows me, why didn't she say anything?"

"Gee, I don't know, because maybe it would ruin your cover," he drawled.

"Oh my God, are we back on the I'm-faking-it thing again?" Ariel snapped. "If you think I'm such a liar, then stop this car."

"Please, like you're going to get out." He slowed to a stop and smirked.

She got out of the car and began to walk.

He kept pace with the windows open so he could talk. "It isn't going to work."

"I can't believe you still think I'm lying."

"That woman knew you."

"If you think that, then why don't you turn that car around and go ask her?" She planted her hands on her hips.

"Maybe I will."

"Do it. I dare you."

Rather than reply, his tires screamed as he u-turned in the road. He drove away, and her shoulders slumped.

He really did think she was a liar. He should also add idiot to that list. She had no idea where she was. No money. Nowhere to go. And she'd pissed off the one person being nice to her.

Not the only one, actually. But she didn't want to ask Pierrot for help.

The noise of the neighborhood surrounded: radios playing clashing songs, people talking, televisions blaring. There were people still outside, leaning against the wall, smoking cigarettes. A man walking his dog.

The footsteps shadowing her.

She was being paranoid again.

Hugging her body, she walked a little faster, and that served as the trigger to have her surrounded by three men, their pants hanging low on their hips, their upper bodies barely covered by tank tops, their inked artwork on display. They smiled at her, one with a gleaming golden tooth. But it wasn't friendly, more in line with a predator about to bite.

"Hey, baby, whatcha doin'?"

The smart thing wasn't to encourage them, and yet her mouth moved before her brain stepped in. "Well, hello there, sugar." The drawl emerged in full force. "I don't suppose you nice boys could help a girl out? I seem to be lost."

One of them straightened his slouch, and surprise

etched is face. "Er, you can come to my place. It's not far."

"That's awfully kind, sugar." She poured on the sweetness. "But I'm just looking for a bit of money to get me a cab and a hotel for the night."

"I know how you can earn it." The one with the golden tooth leered and grabbed. She danced out of reach.

"Not out here." Her heart raced as she did the one thing she knew she shouldn't. She entered a dark alley with three strangers who expected sex.

Surely, she wouldn't do something like that, not even for money. When they crowded close, she wagged a finger. "A woman my age likes to take her time. One at a time," she emphasized. "Don't worry, you'll each get a turn."

It felt as if she watched from outside her body as she led the first of them behind a stack of crates.

The stench of piss rose from the ground. A moment later, the guy who thought he was going first ended up with his face smothered against it. Her body moved without her even thinking, grabbing him by the head and yanking him down to meet the rapid thrust of her knee, his sharp cry covered by her fake moan.

He went limp, and she stood over his slumped frame. Not dead she realized, given his chest rose and fell, but she'd done something to him.

She looked at her hands.

Her killer hands.

Who was she?

A woman about to be in trouble, because she heard one of them shouting. "Hurry up, my balls are gonna burst."

Ariel dropped to her knees, not to help but to rifle through pockets for a bit of change. Not even enough to buy a meal. She grimaced.

She eyed the crates, knowing two more of them stood on the other side.

Could she do it again?

Only one way to find out.

She leaned around the corner and crooked a finger.

The second one came in fast, his lips wet, and his eyes bright. He stumbled on his friend's body, and before he could cry out, her hands were moving again. Too fast for her to grasp. Doing things she was pretty sure she'd never even seen in films. Soon, thug number two landed on his unconscious friend.

Rifling through his pockets, she discovered that he had barely more than the first guy. The third one had enough to maybe get her a room for the night, and she tucked it into her bra before emerging from the alley. She glanced left and right, in time to see low-slung headlights creeping up the street.

The luxury car stopped, and the passenger door opened.

"Get in," Hugo barked.

"Did you get an answer?"

"No."

"Then why come back?"

His gaze locked on hers. "Because I'm a sucker for pain. Get. In."

Rather than tempt the fates, she threw herself into the car. He put it in drive before glancing over at her.

"You're okay? Nothing happened?"

Should she explain that she'd taken out three young men and robbed them, or play dumb? "Lovely night for a walk." Pity, it did nothing for her headache. It throbbed worse than ever.

They spent the rest of the drive in silence and parted ways at the front door. She hurried to her room. Yet closing the door didn't get rid of the tension in her.

She was restless and not the least bit tired. The incident in the alley should have frightened her, made her question what kind of person she was. Yet, adrenaline still coursed through her. She felt...brave.

She exited via the balcony doors, the meek part of her advising that she stay inside where it was safe. But Ariel was beginning to grasp that she was anything *but* meek. The fiery hair should have given that away.

The muggy air moistened her skin, the lack of a breeze not carrying it away. She lifted her face and sucked in a breath as she stared at the stars, so many of them dotting the sky until a cloud passed overhead.

The world grew a bit darker. The lights of the garden provided only dim illumination. They created so many shadows wherein things could hide. She should go back inside. Instead, her feet took her to the pool.

One that had been drained while they were gone and showed brushes at the bottom, along with buckets. Getting resurfaced. The evidence of the death already gone.

She heard music coming from across the way and saw the flicker of a lantern, lit with a flame. Someone was out here.

The hot tub was set into the ground, and so it gave an unobstructed view of the sea. As she neared, she could clearly see the man sitting in it, his bare shoulders jutting up from the edge.

She didn't realize she'd made a sound until Hugo said, "Care to join me?"

"I didn't bring a swimsuit," was her reply, rather than a straight *no*.

"Neither did I."

It was only then that she noticed the pile of clothes by the lantern, the suit he'd worn for their outing in a neatly folded stack.

Again, the right thing to do would be to walk away. To leave this temptation alone.

She still had no idea if she was single or not.

Knew nothing about herself other than the fact that she might just be someone he should be leery of.

Her fingers acted of their own volition, untying the sash that kept the sarong part of the dress closed, then the inner clasp so it could slip off. He didn't turn to look; however, he was aware. She could tell by the rigid set of his shoulders.

Her bra followed the dress, along with her shoes. She kept the thong on. She moved to the steps on his side, rather than those at the far end. There was no handrail to hold onto. She hesitated. What if she slipped?

"Let me help you." He sprang to his feet in the warm water, shock in his gaze, but smoldering admiration, too.

She felt heat flushing her, not in embarrassment. She enjoyed that he stared. Heat blossomed between her legs, starting a dull throb.

He held her hand as she stepped into the hot tub, the water soothing, but not as warm as expected, and fragrant with some kind of scented oil that made her think of spices.

She gasped. "You do know it's cold, right?"

"Refreshing, you mean."

"No, it's cold," she grumbled. Tepid, actually.

"Sorry. The heater is broken. At least, the view is still good."

Once she got past the initial shock, it was pleasant after the muggy heat. Settling onto the molded seat built into the tub, she was treated to a waning moon glittering off the ocean waves, the wispy drift of clouds across shifting the light of it. Soft music played; nothing with words, string instruments with a bit of percussion and piano.

It was soothing. She leaned back with a happy sigh.

"How's your head doing?" he asked.

"How did you know it hurt?" she asked suspiciously. Was he spying on her?

"You kept rubbing your temples in the car."

"Oh." She relaxed. "It's better now." She glanced at him. "Thanks for taking me out of there."

"You saved me having to play nice." He grimaced.

"I thought you knew and liked those people."

"I know some of them," he emphasized. "And even if I knew them all, that's too many at once."

"You don't like crowds?"

"They're not my favorite. I avoid them whenever possible."

"It didn't bother me," she remarked.

"You have an interesting ability to blend in anywhere you need to."

"Maybe I am a spy," she said with a laugh.

"Could be. Although, you mustn't be a very good one."

"What makes you say that?" she huffed, a tad insulted. If he only knew what she'd done in that alley.

"The red hair."

"Are you about to stereotype me?"

"Well, you are quick-tempered."

"Want to see if I can be evil, too?" she grumbled, wondering if he'd fight if she held his head underwater.

"Don't get pissy."

"You're the one who said my red hair makes it unlikely I'm a spy."

His reasoning proved basic. "Red hair like yours would never blend into the background."

"What if my job is to act as bait? Luring people out of hiding."

"To do what? Rob them?"

She thought of the stash of money in her drawer. "Could be I'm a master at espionage."

At that, he snorted. "I still recall you stuck like a fly on the fence."

She splashed him. "Don't remind me."

"You do realize we're debating the unlikely possibility of you being a spy?"

"Hey, a girl needs to work," she joked.

"I know a way to settle this. Let's find out if you can shoot a gun. Because all good spies know how to handle a weapon." He made the water wobble as he stood on the seat and reached for his clothes. The weapon that appeared in his hand widened her eyes.

"You brought a gun to a bachelor party?"

"I bring guns wherever I go, Ariel." He flexed his arms and winked.

She pursed her lips. "You are not funny." But he was cute.

"The truth is, yes, I have a gun. A man in my position never goes out unarmed."

"Is the world that dangerous?"

"I made myself a promise a long time ago to never be a victim."

"By being the perpetrator?" She eyed the weapon.

"Never said I used it. It's more of a backup, a safety net in case I get into a bad situation. Here. See how it feels." The weapon came at her, and she shied away.

"Is it loaded?"

"Kind of useless if it isn't."

"And you're just going to hand it to me?" she said flatly.

"Why not? The safety is on. When you're ready to fire, we'll flip it off."

"It's too dark."

A press of a button fixed that problem. A soft glow illuminated the tub. The clear water showed everything, including his erection.

"Oh." She couldn't look away.

"Is this your way of saying you want to play with a different gun?"

"What? No!" She licked her lips before facing him. "Sorry. That was rude of me. Too much wine."

Hardly, given she'd only had two glasses, and a while ago at that, but he didn't need to know that.

"Here." He pressed her hands around the grip. "Aim it and fire."

"Aim it where?"

"At the moon."

She lifted it, the weight not familiar, and yet she knew how to hold it. Understood the catch on it would release the safety, that she had to keep her arms taut and loose at the same time for the recoil. The pain from the time she'd smashed her nose had taught her a lesson. For a moment, the phantom memory hit her, sharp with pain but no context, no reasoning behind why she'd been firing a gun in the first place.

It faded, and she was left with only the heavy weight of the present and the weapon in her hands. Holding it felt more than passingly familiar to her. It felt right.

And to think he'd handed it to her. What would he think if he knew what'd happened in the alley? Hell, she didn't know what to think. He thought the body that afternoon was an accident. Was it? What if she was a stone-cold killer?

She dropped the gun into the water and watched it sink.

"What did you do that for?" he exclaimed.

"I don't think I like guns."

"Well, I happen to like that one."

"Dry it out, toss it in some rice. I'm sure it will be fine." If taken apart, cleaned and oiled properly.

He eyed her. "If you didn't like it, you could have just handed it back."

"Could have, but didn't. Sorry." Not really. Something about her familiarity with the weapon spooked her.

"Ready to go inside?" he asked.

"Not really, but you can go." She tilted her head to the sky.

"I'm not leaving you out here alone."

"You can't be glued to me forever."

"Nobody wants forever," he said with a grimace.

"No kidding. And yet, look at that couple tonight, wanting to make a go of it. Just the two of them against the world. Don't they know you can only count on yourself?" She didn't know where the bitter words came from.

Yet his reply commiserated. "The only person you can trust is the one you see in the mirror."

Maybe for him, that was true. But in Ariel's case?

"What if you don't recognize them?" And worse, the face looking back scared you?

CHAPTER EIGHTEEN

ARIEL NO SOONER SPOKE, than she tried to stand. Attempted to leave. Embarrassed at the truth she'd allowed to slip. A fear he remembered from a time long ago when his life went to shit, and he'd looked at the face in the mirror and didn't know who it was.

In his case, it was drugs and bad choices that had made him lose sight of himself. It didn't help that he was alone when he really needed was someone to say that he mattered. There was something about despair that made it impossible to see past that moment. To believe there could be something better ahead. It made him speak softly to the woman now struggling to find herself.

"You might not recognize the face right now, but it's still you."

"But who *is* me? And why does the answer to that

scare me?"

"Why would it scare you?"

"Because." She wouldn't look at him as she tried to wade past.

Like fuck. Hugo grabbed for her wrist and held it as he tugged her through the water until she stood between his knees.

She wouldn't meet his gaze.

"Are you really going to act shy now?" he goaded.

Her flashing eyes lifted. "I'm not here to amuse you or satisfy your urge for sarcastic rejoinders."

"Good. Because, otherwise, Gerome might be worried you're coming after his job. The man prides himself on dry comebacks."

"I find him rather witty. Wittier than you."

"But is he as handsome?" Hugo drawled, drawing her closer, noticing how she didn't move away. There was something between them. Something they both kept trying to deny.

"You're a player."

"For all you know, you are, too."

She arched a brow. Rather than be insulted, she sassed right back. "Wouldn't that make me a slut?"

"Slut is a patriarchal term used to remove a woman's power over her own sexuality."

She blinked at him. "Don't tell me you actually believe that?"

"I think it would be hypocritical of me to condemn

a woman for having many partners when that happens to be my preference."

"You'll never settle down?"

"There was a time I might have."

"What happened?"

"She betrayed me. Lied about why she was really in my life. Lied so well, I asked her to marry me."

"Oh."

"I came home early from a business trip and didn't tell her because I wanted it to be a surprise. Only, as it turned out, *I* was the one surprised when I caught her in bed with her lover."

"Oh, Hugo."

It wasn't enough to display his shame; he exposed his bitterness, too. "It's why I know you can't trust anyone but yourself."

"Because those that are supposed to love you most, hurt you the most, too," she said softly.

"What did you remember?"

Her lips flattened into a line. "Something I wish I hadn't."

"Tell me."

She shook her head. "I don't want to. I can't. It's gone."

"Bullshit. Stop playing me. I know you remember more than you're letting on."

"So what if I do? None of what I recall makes sense, and it's like holding onto running water, it slips through the cracks of my mind, leaving me more confused than before."

"Maybe speaking it aloud will clarify it."

"How can I clarify the sight of a child, a boy that I think is my son, being flung into a wall?"

"Why is he being tossed? Who's doing the tossing?"

She shook her head. "I don't know. That's what's so frustrating. I know it's important. But that's all I ever see. That and a man's face. So angry. Hateful."

"And?" Hugo prodded, sensing there was more.

"Blood. On my hands. On the floor." Her voice lowered. "I don't think the body in the pool is the first time I've killed."

"Did it ever occur to you that maybe they deserved it?"

"Does anyone ever deserve to die?"

He could say quite heartily, "Yes. Some people aren't worth the air they breathe."

"Am I one of those people?" She stared at him.

The right answer wasn't the truthful one. "I don't know. A part of me wants to believe and trust you."

"But?"

He shrugged. "I can't." There was something just a bit off about Ariel.

When she went to jerk away, he cajoled, "Come on now, Ariel. Don't be mad. We're just talking."

"No, you're insulting me. Again."

"I have trust issues." He shrugged and offered her a sheepish smile.

"I'm not lying."

"How can I tell for sure, though?"

Her lips quirked. "What if we played a lie detection game."

"I'm surprised you want to mix electronics and water so soon."

Wrong thing to say. Her face paled, and she recoiled.

He hastened to fix the error. "I'm sorry, that was tasteless of me."

Rather than flee, she remained standing by his knees. "Hard to believe that was just this afternoon."

"Given Pierrot never returned, I'd say we're probably in the clear."

"Until the next attack."

She drooped, and he couldn't help but reach for her, drawing her into his lap.

"What are you doing?"

"Can't a man give a sad woman a hug?"

"Your erection is poking me in the bottom."

He grinned. "You're an attractive woman, even when sad."

"And you're handsome, even when I want to throttle you." She turned serious. "You do realize I can't give you anything beyond sex."

"Not asking for anything else."

"I shouldn't even be contemplating it." Her gaze went to his mouth.

How did she drive him crazy with just a look?

"So, we agree to no strings. No regrets. And discretion," he added, more for her benefit.

"What if I'm really bad at it and can't remember how?"

His lips quirked. "Then you can sing that Madonna song."

The jest had her laughing. "Oh, I doubt I'm a virgin." She giggled. "What if I don't know how to please you?"

"Don't you get it? You already please me. Hell, all you have to do is say '*hello*,' and I get hard."

The right reply, apparently, because her lips were suddenly on his. A hot clash of flesh and breath as his arms closed around her, reveling in the feel of her so close. She didn't move out of his grip but rather straddled him instead, the core of her sitting on his thighs, her hands cupping his cheeks, her kiss passionate and skilled.

And to think she'd been afraid. She kissed him as if he were a precious treat. She sucked on his tongue in a way that made his cock jealous. She squirmed in his lap and almost made a grown man embarrass himself.

Almost. She wasn't the only one with talent. He broke the embrace to nip his way along her jaw to her ear. Teasing the lobe and shell of it as she squirmed and panted for him.

But he wasn't done. He cupped her breasts with his hands, weighing their natural heaviness, squeezing them and watching through half-slit eyes as she sighed and leaned her head back. Letting herself bask in the pleasure.

There was more to come. He bent her even farther and leaned forward so that he might brush his mouth across the tip of one breast, then the other, the slight stubble on his jaw creating friction against her delicate skin.

Ariel shivered. "Again."

He rubbed across the other erect tip and then followed with his lips. She moaned and ground herself against his lap.

He opened his mouth and flicked her nipple with the tip of his tongue.

She gasped.

He did it again. Teasing her before he truly licked the areola. He teased those hardened berries until she panted. "I think you made me come a little."

"Don't come too much yet, we're not done," he growled, suctioning his mouth around her breast, tugging it hard, and grazing it with his teeth.

She uttered a deep groan that shot pleasure right to his dick.

She grabbed his hair and dug her fingers in, riding his thighs as he kept teasing her tips.

He thought about seeing if he could make her

come just by sucking and biting her breasts, but he had to see. Had to know.

He lifted her until she sat on the edge of the hot tub, that ridiculous scrap of material hiding her pubes.

Tearing them free showed him nothing.

As in not a single hair. Bare. The waxed kind that didn't leave even stubble.

"Disappointed?" she said huskily.

"The mystery of your true hair color remains." He placed a kiss on the nude skin.

"How about a consolation prize?"

When she parted her thighs, he saw heaven.

He lost all finesse as he fell on her, his tongue reaching out to lap at her sweet core. He groaned at the taste of her. And when the vibration of that sound brought a sharp cry from her lips, he made another noise and dug his fingers in to hold her in place.

He wasn't about to miss this feast.

His tongue didn't just part her lips, it stroked against her swollen clit. He alternated—a flick of her button, then diving in with his tongue until she thrashed in his grip.

"Yes. Yes," she chanted, just the one word, over and over.

He was more than happy to oblige...with one caveat. He wasn't letting her come on his tongue. He sat on the ledge beside her, the shaped concrete biting into his ass, but better his skin than hers as he drew her onto his lap. She straddled him without words, her hand guiding the head of him into her.

The heat and way she gripped him had him fighting to not simply plunge inside.

She squirmed against him, driving him deep. "Don't get shy now, sugar," she murmured against his mouth.

He needed no more motivation. Hands gripping her ass, he pumped, thrust in and out, feeling how she tightened around him, loving how she embraced him in her arms. And cried his name as she came.

Came hard on him, just as he came hard in her.

Without a condom, which did a lot to ensure that he didn't linger inside her body. In a moment, he had them both back in the tub, rinsing away his loss of control, and then compounding it by feathering her lips and face with soft kisses.

They didn't say much. Words might have ruined the mood. May have brought the regret a little too soon. There was time enough in the morning, in the light of day, to wonder about what they'd done.

He held Ariel's hand as he walked her back to her room. He waited to see if she'd invite him in.

Instead, she gave him a shy smile. "Thanks. See you in the morning."

That was all she had to say?

She closed the patio door, and the curtain swished shut.

He stared at it a moment.

No strings. He'd said it himself. So, why did he expect—no, make that *want*—more?

He didn't. Blame the stupid, romantic night.

Returning to his office where he kept the best scotch, he'd barely taken a sip when he realized he wasn't alone.

CHAPTER NINETEEN

ARIEL FLOATED TO BED. Her body felt good. Her mind, not as anxious. Sex had helped her find a mellow place that had her hitting the pillow with a soft sigh.

It evaporated the moment someone barged into her room.

Instinct meant that she screamed and threw a pillow, which resulted in an incredulous female voice saying, "That was seriously the worst toss I've ever seen you do."

She blinked and regarded the intruder. The woman seemed familiar, and not just because she'd seen her earlier that night.

"What are you doing here? Who are you?"

"No need to play for the cameras, Merry. They've been taken offline. We came the moment we realized you were in trouble."

"Wait. What?" She pushed up from the bed, all

trace of sleep gone from her system. "Do you know me?" Odd how she didn't feel even one bit worried, despite the intrusion.

The query brought a strange twist to the intruder's lips. "Is that a rhetorical question?"

"I don't know who I am."

"You better not be fucking with me, Meredith."

The name...it sounded right and wrong all at once. She heard another one in her head, *Anita Whittaker*. And then more. *Madeline Parker. Josephine Walker.*

How could she know what was real?

"I don't recognize that name."

"What?" The woman stared at her. "Are you high?"

She frowned. "I've not taken any drugs, no. But I did suffer a bump to the head that left me bereft of my identity."

"Bullshit," the woman with the tanned skin muttered. "Wait, you're serious?"

Ariel nodded. "Mr. Laurentian, the owner of this house, found me on the beach and ensured I got help. But the hospital couldn't do anything for me. They say my memory will come back when it's ready."

"Daaaaamn." The Latina-appearing female drew out the word. "So, you really don't remember a thing? What name are you using, then?"

"For the moment, I am using Ariel. Hugo helped me choose it."

"Ariel?" The woman's left brow arched. "I am going to throat punch the bastard."

"Why?"

"Because he named you after a cartoon mermaid."

"It was better than Jane." Her lips twisted with the wry reply.

"Did you really forget it all? It seems so impossible, especially since Mother seemed to think you were supposed to be here with him."

"Mother? Are we sisters?"

"We're closer than sisters," the woman exclaimed, the vehemence in the statement warming Ariel for some reason. "I can't believe you don't know who I am."

"I'm sorry." Ariel shook her head. "Is that why you were staring at me in the club and came to find me on the sidewalk?"

"Well, yeah. We're friends."

"Why didn't you say so before?"

"Because I figured you had a reason for pretending."

"Have we known each other a long time?"

"About ten years, give or take. Close enough that you're part of my wedding party."

"I am?"

"Kind of in charge of the whole thing too, so if you're not screwing with me, then this memory thing might put a crimp in the plans."

Ariel's mouth rounded into an O of surprise. "I'm a wedding planner?"

"On occasion. But more like...office coordinator and welcoming committee. We work together."

"Doing what?"

The woman's face grew guarded. "Interior design and realty projects."

"Oh." Her lips turned down. "That's less interesting than expected."

"What did you expect?"

She didn't tell the woman about her fantasy of being some jet-setting woman of the world. It was ridiculous. Interior design sounded like fun.

"My name is Tanya." The woman held out her hand.

"Tanya," Ariel repeated, but something about that name didn't fit, didn't sound right. Did the woman lie? "And you say my name is Meredith?"

"Merry to your friends. Do you remember your kids?"

"My babies," Ariel whispered, her voice choking. "Donovan and..." She paused. Her brow crinkled, and while she could see a chubby-cheeked face, she couldn't put a name to it. "I can't remember." Her voice broke.

"Caroline," Tanya said softly.

"They must be so worried. Who is watching them?"

"Your kids are both in their twenties and moved

out. They're fine. I don't think they know you're missing yet. But they'll notice after the wedding if you don't go back home."

"Wait, aren't you getting married tomorrow?" Ariel's eyes widened.

"No. And a good thing, too, because you sound like you might need some help remembering shit."

"How are you going to help me?"

"I don't know. But good thing you've got a bunch of friends who'll want to help. Tanya lifted her wrist to her mouth and spoke. "Ladies, we have a problem."

20

INTERLUDE: PASS THE WHISKEY

TANYA LET the man pour himself a shot of scotch. The good stuff. She'd already rifled through his bottles of booze and his drawers where she found the hand-rolled cigars. Tanya pocketed a pair for Devon, along with a sticky pad and pen. She always ran out of them.

Even rumpled, Mr. Hugo Laurentian was handsome. She watched him from behind the curtain, a seemingly dumb yet effective way of hiding in plain sight. The trick was to be slimmer than the fabric. Devon complained good-naturedly about his broad shoulders, making it impossible for him to turn sideways and disappear. She liked those shoulders quite a bit, even if they meant leaving him behind for this mission. Given they required subtlety and stealth, and he was a guy, he was back at the resort. But he didn't go willingly.

"You do realize sending you off into possible danger is emasculating to the extreme?" he'd said.

Devon hated it when he couldn't be a hero. Even though they'd been dating a few months, he still felt a need to impress her.

It was cute.

She'd kissed him and said, "I'll be back before dawn."

This was a mission for moms only. The earpiece she wore whispered. "I am now in full control of the cameras inside the house. You are clear. Target is alone." Audrey was running tech support for the mission.

From Louisa, "Roger that. The big dude in the suit has gone to his room and turned off the lights."

Tanya kept quiet because the curtain wouldn't stop sound.

The patio door was unlocked. The office one would only take a few seconds to pop if he'd engaged it. But this was an operation that required they exert caution and refrain from causing harm—unless he gave them cause.

This was an unsanctioned intel mission. Mother would have a kitten when she found out. But they were willing to accept the consequences. Mr. Hugo Laurentian needed to fess up to what he was doing that had Meredith behaving so oddly.

The man leaned back in his chair and sipped the

scotch before saying, "Are you waiting for anything in particular before you pop out and yell '*boo*?'"

Tanya said nothing, even as she wondered who he spoke to. Audrey muttered in her ear. "I think he's talking to you."

"I know you're behind the curtain. Might as well show yourself."

Louisa, who heard it all, cursed. "Fuck. You're busted. I'm coming."

"Going to say hello," she hissed before stepping out into the open. She smiled at Mr. Hugo Laurentian, the first. Preliminary digging showed no family attached to him. No living relatives, nor a past they could dig into. For all intents and purposes, he came into existence about seventeen years ago.

Which made him a person of interest, especially once Mother pulled them aside at the club and ordered them not to pay him any attention.

As if that would happen. They'd all seen Meredith sporting a puzzled expression at the bachelor party, one that had turned into a Jack and Jill. If this were a mission, Meredith never would have agreed to go, because she would have worried about blowing her cover.

Not only that, Merry never acknowledged them. Not even with a blink.

It was risky to the extreme, but even when under deep, they always managed a little something to convey that they were safe, or a tell that said, "*get me the hell out*." While doing her short stint on stage, Carla kept flashing the are-you-okay sign.

Meredith either ignored it, or...something was wrong.

"Would you like a glass?" Hugo the first tilted his tumbler towards the decanter.

"She'd prefer the whiskey you've got hiding," Louisa announced, slipping through the patio door, gun out, but at least she wasn't firing. Tanya and the others had done a few missions with the petite woman known under the codename Dance Mom. It ran in the family, apparently, given that her daughter ended up going to Juilliard.

Even with a gun trained on him, the man didn't so much as flinch. Just reached for two glasses on the tray that had started out with four. "I'm afraid I didn't think to grab any ice."

"That's fine, I take mine neat," Louisa remarked, moving farther into the room, her steps a thing of grace, her tight, dancer's body able to contort in ways that made everyone envious. It came in handy with booby-trapped spaces.

Audrey said just one thing in her ear. "Door."

It meant Tanya moved to grab something from the desk, drawing his eye, while Louisa shifted, covering the opening of the door. By the time everyone had stopped moving, and Portia had taken up a spot, there were three killers in the room.

Still, he wasn't sweating.

It made Louisa grumble. "Should have brought more guns."

Mother wouldn't let them carry anything big between missions. It didn't stop them from buying stuff on their own, but their personal stashes were back home. Damned airlines had such a hissy fit when they found munition aboard, not that they ever suspected the sweet, blond lady in economy thirteen-A. Tanya had felt bad that time they dragged a guy off, screaming that he was innocent.

"Have a seat, ladies. I assume you're here about the contract on my life." He gestured to the pair of chairs.

It was Louisa who exclaimed, "Wait a second, you've got a hit out on you?"

Tanya was just as surprised. She spoke aloud to Audrey. "Did you hear that?"

"I did, checking it out."

"Ask Mason, it might be quicker," Tanya muttered. She recalled seeing him chatting with their current target.

"Mason had too much sun and drink. He's passed out, but don't worry, I've already got the info."

"Spill it," Tanya said, not even bothering to hide the fact that she was wired.

"Not much to say, other than someone put out a notice on the dark web that Mr. Laurentian was worth ten million dead."

"Ten million!" Louisa exclaimed, drawing his attention. "How come we're not doing this job?"

"Who says we aren't?" Portia retorted. "Or have you forgotten why we're here?"

Could the hit be the reason Mother had told them to stay away? Had they just ruined Merry's mission?

Tanya shook her head. "Something's not right. She wouldn't have ghosted us for a hit."

He finally frowned. "If you're not here because of the contract for my death, then why *are* you here?"

"You have a friend of ours staying with you," Tanya stated, still wondering at his lack of fear or worry. A man who thought three women had come to kill him shouldn't be so calm.

"Ah, now it's becoming clear." He poured some whiskey and handed them out. Only Portia turned it down. "So, you know who my mysterious guest is."

"We know her very well, in fact. But you are a bit of an enigma." They'd not had much time between the club and their infiltration of his property to find out much. Tanya pulled out her large-screen phone. She began to read. "Hugo Laurentian, dual citizen of both the United States and the Bahamas. Yet you sport a distinctly French accent as if you spent your developing years elsewhere. The *elsewhere* being blank as there is no record of your actual birth."

"Would it help if I said my mother was French?" Hugo offered with a charming smile.

"And your father?"

He shrugged. "No idea. My mother wasn't particular about her paramours."

"How did you get so rich?" Louisa wandered the room, not willing to sit down. The glass of liquor in her hand showed no signs of being drunk but would make a fabulous missile if launched.

"I invested well."

"But where did that initial funding come from?"

"A misspent youth. Now that I've answered some questions, your turn. How do you know Ariel?" he riposted, his eyes two calculating stones.

"Who is Ariel?" Louisa asked, pausing to look over her shoulder away from the large piece of art on the wall.

"The only Ariel I know is a mermaid princess," Portia stated.

Tanya leaned forward from the armrest she perched on. "When you say 'Ariel,' do you mean the redhead you brought to a stripper party?"

"Nobody actually stripped," he reminded.

"But you brought her expecting it!" Louisa jabbed a finger at him.

"Actually, I brought her knowing it would be crashed."

"How did you meet?" Tanya asked.

"Didn't your research tell you about the woman I found on the beach? As an honest citizen of the island, I immediately provided aid. And when the hospital would have discharged her to the streets, still lacking an identity or means of caring for herself, I offered the use of my home.

Look up the police report. It should all be in there."

Audrey was the one to quickly brief her. "There is no police report."

Tanya said nothing aloud because he seemed rather certain, meaning either he lied, or he didn't. In which case, the story was part of Merry's cover.

"Where is Merry right now?"

"In her room, sleeping, I imagine. Or is she? It would seem I've been fooled. Exactly who are you, and who is Ariel?"

"Ariel?" Louisa snickered.

"She claimed to not know her name, so I helped her choose one," he said with a shrug.

"Wait just a second," Louisa exclaimed. "You mean to say you named her after a cartoon?"

He shrugged. "It seemed apt at the time."

"Let's go back to the amnesia thing. That doesn't sound like something Merry would do," Portia murmured.

"I should have known she was lying."

"What makes you think she's not telling the truth?" Tanya queried because a loss of memory would explain Merry's odd behavior.

"Because it's so blatantly something out of a soap opera. I knew she had to be faking."

"Yet you took her into your home."

He eyed Tanya over the rim of his glass. "She was interesting."

"Do you always bring *interesting* things home?"

"No." Said tersely. "And I am reminded why." He eyed them one by one. "You were all at the party, meaning you are acquainted with some of the same people I know. People with..." He paused. "Interesting careers."

A polite way of putting it. "Do the initials KM mean anything to you?" Tanya asked.

He shook his head.

"What about Bad Boy Inc.?"

"They handle all my realty needs."

"Ever hire them for non-property deals?" Louisa queried.

He leaned back in his chair. "When are we going to get frank here?"

"Depends, when are you going to admit that you're not the aboveboard businessman you'd like us to believe?"

"Never claimed I was." The wide smile again was much too engaging. No wonder Merry was attracted.

"You need to cut to the chase," Audrey announced. "There's a vehicle approaching the gate."

Tanya turned serious. "Merry is part of a secret agency that is similar to Bad Boy."

"But with better taste," Louisa said, rubbing the fabric of his curtains between her fingers.

"Wait a second." He snapped his fingers. "You're the all-female agency. Mothers only, right? I've heard of you."

"Then you know we're not to be messed with," Louisa stated, suddenly twirling a knife.

"If you've done anything to Merry, now is the time to admit it," Tanya said.

"Um, guys..." Audrey's voice sounded hesitant. "You might want to stand down."

Rather than reply, she eyed Hugo. "Swear you did nothing to Merry."

"I can assure you, I did nothing to Ariel." His expression soured.

"Bullshit," Louisa exclaimed. "Admit it, you knew she was faking and punished her. Was it a drug? Did you dope her to make her your little sex toy?"

"Anything we did was with full consent."

"Oh my God, you slept with her. Thinking she had amnesia." Portia shook her head in disgust.

Whereas Tanya proved pragmatic. "Who wouldn't sleep with Merry when she decides she wants it?"

"You needn't worry, it will never happen again." His expression turned quite grim. "I won't be played. Now, if you're done, take your lying friend and leave."

The man was genuinely pissed that he'd been fooled, but Tanya had to wonder. What if Merry told the truth?

The moment she thought it, she heard Carla in her ear. "We have a problem."

"What kind?" she asked.

"The kind that needs you, pronto."

Tanya eyed the other moms.

"You go see Carla while Portia and I keep an eye on Mr. Laurentian."

"Make it fast," Audrey hissed. "I just lost control of the cameras. And that car I was telling you about just pulled up."

"Incoming," Tanya announced. "Head out, don't engage. I'll go see what the hold-up is with Carla and Merry."

Heading into the hall, she had no time to admire the grandeur of the house. With Audrey losing the link to the security system, they were now moving around blind. The good news was that Laurentian seemed reasonable. They'd seen nothing that indicated violence on his part. But she'd met monsters before who could hide their true natures.

Given the clock ticked, she ran, knowing where to find Carla given they'd studied the floorplan of the mansion before infiltration. At the door with its scalloped design, she engaged in a brisk knocking—rapid three, pause, hard knock, rapid four.

The door swung open to Carla's scowl.

"What's the problem? Did you not find Merry?"

"I found her, all right." Carla jerked her head. "Except she doesn't know she's Merry on account she lost her memory."

"I just heard." A piece of intel that might have been useful beforehand, and yet, apparently, someone tried to cover it up. The lack of a police report was particularly damning. Why cover it up?

"Because she doesn't know who I am, not even her name, she's refusing to come with me."

Glancing past Carla, Tanya noted Merry pacing by the bed, wearing a nightgown with a robe loosely belted over it.

"Merry, you have to come with us. We can't leave you here."

That brought a crease to Merry's brow. "I can't just leave. It's the middle of the night, and I don't know you. Either of you." Her arms wrapped around her torso, and Tanya could see the trepidation tensing her body.

She truly appeared afraid. "I swear to you, Meredith, you know us. Me. I'm Tanya, a—" she started to say, only to have Merry interrupt.

"No, you're not, because she's..." Merry turned a grimace on Carla. "Dammit. You lied to me. Tanya isn't your real name."

"Just testing," Carla said with an unapologetic shrug.

"We don't have time for this. We have to go. Mr. Laurentian is about to get some company."

"Who? Are they armed?" Carla asked, her expression brightening.

"Don't know. Audrey lost the link." Usually, Tanya was the one manning the tech part of the missions, but given Audrey's recent condition, she'd been pulled from field duty.

"Armed? Who the hell are you guys?" Merry gasped.

"Again, I'm Tanya." She pointed to herself.

"If you're Tanya, then who is she?" Merry pointed.

"Carla. The bride who is about to go loco if we don't get out of here and fix this." Carla was losing patience.

It wasn't helping the situation.

Merry hugged herself tighter, shrugging her shoulders inward. "You can't fix this. I really can't remember you, or anything."

"Which is scary, I'm sure. But you can't stay here," Tanya said softly.

"I have nowhere else to go."

"Of course, you do," Carla exploded. "You have a home. Two, actually, given you bought that condo in Florida for the winter months. Not to mention you came with like six suitcases, which are still sitting in your suite. I knew there was something wrong when your collection of makeup and shit was still in your bathroom."

Along with all her identification and her specials toys—not the vibrating kind. Her lipstick that acted as a transmitter. The pen that could emit acid to burn through a lock. The necklace and pendant that could act as a garrote and one-time-use Taser.

"Am I really that vain?" Merry asked with a wrinkle of her nose.

"You are awesome. And we'll tell you all about yourself once we're out of here."

"But, Hugo..." Meredith chewed her lower lip, and it struck Tanya in that instant that she looked soft. Womanly. A different version of the Merry they knew that brimmed with confidence and sexuality. A woman who used and discarded men.

Was this how she could have been if she'd not been so sorely used and abused?

Moving towards her, Tanya clasped her hands. "Look at me."

It took a moment.

"I realize this might seem rather frightening, but you have to believe me when I say you don't belong here."

"No, you are the ones who shouldn't be here. What are you doing meddling?" Mother exclaimed as she barged into the room with an entourage at her back. She arrived with a seething Hugo, the less-than-amused butler slash right-hand man, and Louisa and Portia.

Mother looked pissed.

"Merry needed us," Carla stated.

"No, she didn't," Mother snapped. "I told you specifically to stay away from Laurentian."

"You did." Carla didn't even disagree.

"And you ignored me?" Mother said with an arched brow that never boded well during their training camp.

"We had to when Merry didn't reply to the hand signal." Carla was matter-of-fact.

Tanya hopped in to help. "I agree, we had to. Or have we suddenly changed the rules?" The most basic one being: leave no mother or child behind.

Mother's lips pursed. "Thing is, she couldn't respond because she doesn't remember it."

The implication proved explosive. "Hold on a second, you knew she lost her memory!" Carla was shocked.

"How could you?" Tanya squeaked. Poor Merry's eyes were so wide. She said not a word, just appeared to soak in the argument.

Mother finally looked chagrinned. "To be honest, at first, I thought she was using an amnesia ploy as a way to get close to her target."

All eyes went to Hugo, who had a deadly glint in his eyes.

The words emerged tight and clipped from his lips. "Get close so she could kill me, you mean."

At that, Mother laughed. "Oh no, not kill. On the contrary, we were hired to keep you alive."

CHAPTER TWENTY-ONE

ARIEL, who apparently had the real name of *Meredith*, was feeling more confused by the second. First, she had been awoken by a stranger who claimed to know her and thought she faked losing her memories. Gave her a false name, too. Then the real Tanya appeared, followed by even more people, shoving their way inside her room. That lady Marie from the club, Gerome, two more strangers, and Hugo.

An angry Hugo. The tautness of his body spread from head to toe. His gaze did not meet hers. But she couldn't help but stare at him.

Did he understand as little as she did about the situation? She'd tried to follow it, but there was talk of people being armed, then some kind of wild accusation that she would actually lie to get close to Hugo. But that wasn't the most shocking thing. Something else jumped out at her from that information overload.

"Hold on a second, did you say someone is trying to kill Hugo?" To her, that seemed the most important question to ask.

"Many someones more than likely, given the payout," Carla stated.

She blinked in her direction. "Payout? I don't understand." This all seemed so crazy and far-fetched, yet no one in the room seemed fazed by it at all.

Marie, no longer wearing the vivid red dress of earlier, appeared less angry than when she arrived but still quite stern, except when she looked at Ariel. She reached for Ariel's hands, her grip firm and drawing her gaze.

"No need to be frightened. This memory-loss thing is surely temporary. You'll be yourself in no time."

"And who is that, exactly?"

"We'll tell you later."

Ariel pulled her hands free. "How about right now? Because I don't even know if I want to go anywhere with you. You all sound like you're crazy killers or something."

"Not for this job. We were security detail for this one," Carla stated. "Actually, you were. Which reminds me, given we were all here, why the heck didn't you recruit any of us to help her?" Said to Marie.

"Merry didn't want anyone distracted from the wedding." Marie shrugged. "She wanted it to be perfect." A glance at Carla had her looking bashful.

"Here's the thing I don't understand about your

bullshit story," Hugo snapped. "I never hired your agency to protect me. Not to mention, I didn't even know about the hit on my life until after I met your spy." The last word was spat in Ariel's direction.

It took a bit more will than expected not to flinch at the vehemence. It would serve no purpose to claim that she didn't know anything. It would seem this Meredith, this Merry, could be an accomplished liar.

"I am not a spy," Ariel couldn't help but exclaim. "I don't know these people. I have no idea what they're talking about."

"Drop the fucking act."

"We'll explain everything once we get out of here." The one called Tanya, the real one, grabbed her hand and squeezed it in comfort.

"You'll explain why first," Hugo demanded.

Marie answered. "A mutual friend asked a favor."

"What friend would—? Doesn't matter." He swore and rubbed his face. Then he glared at Gerome. "Did you know about all this?"

"It was only after the party that the connection was made."

"And you didn't think to tell me that our guest was a spy?" Hugo never once looked at her.

Ariel's heart shrank. So much for the intimacy of earlier.

"She wasn't here to hurt you." Gerome shifted.

"You were never even supposed to know we were involved," Marie interjected.

"Kind of hard to ignore once she took over my guest bedroom." The look he sent her way shriveled her.

"Which wasn't supposed to happen. Obviously, her injury and memory loss couldn't be predicted."

"And it's just a coincidence that she ended up on my beach?" He snorted. "I'm not stupid. I am also done with this clusterfuck of people in my house. It is four in the morning. I want some sleep."

"Which is our cue to leave," Carla stated.

"Wait." It was Ariel/Merry who saw a problem. "If someone is trying to kill Hugo, and you were hired to protect him, shouldn't someone stay here to do that?"

Marie glanced at Hugo.

He said nothing, but the expression said it all.

"I think Mr. Laurentian would prefer to arrange his own security."

When Hugo spoke, it was to make a flat demand. "I'll expect a full accounting of what you have discovered thus far so that I can continue the search into the person funding my ten-million-dollar demise. You will also send me the bill rather than this...friend."

"No charge." Marie waved a hand. "But I will extend an apology for disrupting you. I'll have a chat with my daughters about their disobedience and rash decision-making."

The women all winced, whereas Merry felt confused. Was this Marie their boss or parent? Eyeing her, neither seemed quite right. Only one word came to mind: *friend*.

"Under the circumstances, I think it best if I abstain from attending the wedding." He glanced at Carla. "I'll figure out some apology for Philip."

The reminder brought a scowl to Carla. "Don't you even think of pulling that on me a few days before the wedding. If Philip invited you, then it's because he values you. And I'll be damned if you don't show up because one of your friends hired us and then shit happened. Get it under control!" Carla snapped before stalking out.

The woman closest to the door gasped, whereas Tanya offered, "She's under a lot of stress."

"Meaning you'd better show up, or she'll shoot you for free," stated a woman with a trim figure and her hair pulled back in a tight bun.

For some reason, Ariel/Merry suddenly saw the same woman, but in a leotard, leaping across a stage then spinning to kick someone in the face.

She blinked, and it was gone. The lithe woman left with the other one whose name she'd never gotten, leaving only Tanya and Marie. As for Gerome, he followed them. That must mean that he didn't consider those that remained a threat.

Idiot.

Another stray thought blinked through, and it meant she missed part of the conversation and caught it at—

"...get your security to confer with ours to avoid an incident."

"I won't bring any to the wedding itself. Just expect Gerome to be around somewhere on the resort grounds. After all, there will be more agents at this wedding than I could ever think of hiring."

It made Meredith wonder who Carla was marrying. Was it like a *Mr. and Mrs. Smith* thing? Spy marrying spy?

"Sounds good. Come along, ladies." Marie left the room, but Tanya hesitated, waiting on Merry.

"If I could have a moment with Hugo, please."

"We have nothing to say," he growled. But at least he remained, his face a dark mask. Furious. No sign of the soft and gentle lover of before.

"Yell if you need anything," Tanya stated, leaving the room.

Merry waited a moment before starting with a hesitant, "I'm—"

"Don't you dare give me some fake apology."

"I had no idea."

He snorted. "I highly doubt that. Maybe you've got them fooled, but I'm not playing your game."

"It's not a game."

"You're right, it's not. What you are is a lie. And I want you gone."

CHAPTER TWENTY-TWO

HUGO COULD SEE he'd hurt her. The words practically slapped her with their viciousness and did nothing to ease his pride. His anger at being duped.

And still she played. Pretended the innocence, the lack of memory.

Did she take him for a fool?

"Was the sex part of your mission to get close to me?"

"My what?"

"You know, the one to cozy up and murder me."

"You heard them. My mission was to protect."

"As if they'd admit anything else." He sneered. He didn't understand why the betrayal stung so badly. He barely knew the woman. Had expected perfidy from the beginning. It would have been nice to be wrong for once.

"Forget them. I'm not going to kill you."

"As if you'd admit it out loud."

"Why are you being like this?"

"Being what? Normal? How else should I react now that I know you've been using me?"

"Use you for what? You're being irrational. I have no idea what's going on. I can't even tell if those women are telling the truth."

"Oh, they are. They're exactly who they say they are."

"A protection agency of women for hire?" The laughter sounded almost bitter. "Do you even realize how ridiculous that sounds? I wish I was that exciting. The tanned one also told me I'm some kind of interior designer."

A pity that wasn't the real her. As a man who bought and sold properties after flipping them, a partner with those skills would have been a perfect match. "Which is your cover, obviously."

"Paint splotches and fabrics swathes are a far cry from murdering people. I don't think I could do it." She put a hand on her stomach and looked pale.

He didn't fall for it. "It's time you left."

"It doesn't feel right leaving like this."

"How else should it feel? We both knew this situation was never permanent, even before the lies."

"I don't even know where I'm supposed to go."

"I'm sure your friends can show you the room at the resort where they've been staying." Each word tasted bitter in his mouth.

"Will I see you again?"

"I said I'd be at the wedding." Unless he could find a polite way to extricate himself without setting off the bride.

"I mean before that. Once we've both had a chance to sleep and stuff."

"Why? There's nothing left to say, or—" His gaze flicked to her frame, and he purposely made his disdain drip as he said, "Do."

Color in her cheeks had her exclaiming, "Then I guess this is goodbye."

"And good riddance," he muttered.

"Now you're just being plain mean." She whirled away from him, tears hinting in her eyes and thick, choked words.

How dare she cry?

A part of him wanted to chase after her as she left. He'd been cruel. In his pain, he'd lashed out. It seemed unfair that he now suffered guilt and wanted to apologize.

Gerome found him in his office, a glass of scotch in hand, leaning back in his chair, replaying the footage of his home being overrun.

He pointed to the screen. "They are damned good."

"Not that good. They set off my alarm." Gerome shook his wristwatch.

"They were in my office before you knew, though. Had they been actual killers, you'd be looking for another job."

The big man harrumphed and scowled. "If you'd let me hire more people like I asked..."

"Then I'd have them constantly underfoot. I was perfectly fine."

"You don't look fine," Gerome stated. "For what it's worth, she really did lose her memory. Her friends were incredibly concerned about her after they saw her at the club."

"Even if the amnesia is real, it doesn't change who she is."

"I didn't take you for a snob."

"It has nothing to do with snobbery. Just plain facts. She is not who she claimed to be. And given the problem, is best off with her friends. Not here."

Not with him.

Once Gerome left, grumbling something about a stronger firewall, Hugo kept replaying the videos. Especially the one of her confronting the other woman with a pillow.

The confusion on her face.

The shock.

He even watched himself being cold to her. Saw once more how she shrank with each cruel word.

Finally, he watched the camera at the gate where she glanced back in the direction of the house before she got into a car.

The vehicle left the property, and he watched long past the taillights disappeared, long enough that he saw someone step into the space in front of the gate.

What the fuck?

He leaned forward and stared. Rewound and stared some more.

Someone definitely stood outside the gate and then started to climb it.

Rather than call Gerome, he opened his desk drawer and armed himself. Then he took the golf cart to the gates, the bottle of solvent on the seat beside him.

When he arrived, the climber dangled, the early morning sun catching them in its rays.

Exiting the cart, Hugo took his time sauntering over.

He glanced up at the person and smiled. "Allo. Are you lost?"

A dark gaze met his, and the person struggled. Cursing.

"I wouldn't bother. You'll just get caught worse. Now, be a good *garcon* and stop wiggling, will you? I'm going to get you down, and then you and I will have a chat."

Only that chat never happened because who should happen along at that early hour, but the super-intendent himself.

His police car slowed to a halt outside the gates, and Hugo held in a sigh as he climbed down.

Pierrot emerged from the driver's seat and drawled.

"Looks like I visited at just the right time. You've got a trespasser."

"Who was about to explain why he's here."

"As if you don't know. My girlfriend is missing."

For a moment, he actually wondered if he spoke of Ariel, but the man was much too young and unrefined for someone like her.

It was Pierrot who drew the right conclusion. "Five foot five, dark hair, about shoulder-length, tattoo of a bird on her hip?"

"Yeah. Did you arrest her?"

"Not exactly. You need to come with me." A stream of curse words not in French or English emerged. Pierrot didn't pay it any mind and was ready when the solution did its job and dumped the fellow.

The cuffs went on, despite a slight scuffle, and before Hugo could find out anything, Pierrot hustled the man off.

But that wasn't what required several glasses of scotch to fall asleep.

Ariel.

Dammit.

Why did she have to betray him?

CHAPTER TWENTY-THREE

THE LAST WORDS she'd had with Hugo pressed heavily on her. She had little to say on the drive back to the resort, but the other women never shut up. She discovered all their names. Louisa, Audrey, and Portia rode with her, while the other vehicle held Tanya, Carla, and Marie. Marie Cadeaux, whom everyone called Mother.

She finally asked. "Did she adopt you all or something?"

"She's not our mother-mother." Tanya practically rolled her eyes. "She's our handler. Your handler too when you go in the field."

"Handler. As in a spy on a mission?" So much to understand, and none of it rang any bells.

"Depends on the job. You're versatile."

"Almost as flexible as Louisa is," Audrey joked.

"Don't stress trying to remember," Portia soothed.

"It will come back eventually."

"You can't know that for sure," Merry argued, the name feeling right and wrong at once. Was it wrong she still wanted to be Ariel?

"Seeing your things might spark it."

Except seeing the beautiful clothes in the closet did not make her recall buying them. Nor did the long line of toiletries do more than make her wonder how much time she spent daily in the bathroom.

The stories shared only served to make her feel even more alienated than before.

The person they described seemed so different. Brave and self-assured for starters. A bit of a slut, too, by all accounts.

"How many husbands have I had?" she asked, sure she'd misunderstood.

"Six, but you didn't consummate four of those on account that they were old. One died right after the wedding."

"I killed him?" she squeaked.

"Heart attack."

It stunned to know she'd married a few times in the name of getting the job done. None of them very long marriages, thankfully. Apparently, she didn't like being separated from her children for long.

She had babies. Not so young anymore, though. Their image on her phone had her touching the screen, sad, mostly because they seemed familiar yet she couldn't recall their youth.

She'd had to research to find out even their middle names.

It hurt to know she'd forgotten her own children.

She spent the day in her room, which didn't prove very restful given someone kept checking on her every few hours. Did they think she'd run away?

Even Jacques showed up. Seeing him outside her door, she chose to slip out into the hall rather than invite him in.

"Superintendent," she said, adopting Hugo's word for him. "I'm surprised to see you here."

"I went to check on you at Mr. Laurentian's. However, he informed me your friends came to fetch you. I take it you've remembered everything?" His gaze was intent.

She shook her head. "Not yet, but I'm sure it won't be long."

"I do hope you'll keep me informed. I want to see you recover."

"Thank you."

"I had another reason for visiting. So, we got a lead on the person who drowned in the pool. Turns out they're not actually from here. They flew in from Chicago." He said it as if it should mean something.

"And?"

"Isn't that where you're from?"

"No idea. Should I dig out my driver's license to see? I'm sure it's around here somewhere." She'd come across her identification as she rifled through every single possession. She recalled staring at the picture of a serious-faced her, and an age that seemed a few years younger than expected. Was she really only thirty-four? Because she'd have said early forties, at least.

"I will need a copy of it for our records. But back to the person in the pool. Turns out they were wanted by your American law enforcement."

"For what?" she exclaimed.

"Assault and battery. Theft over five thousand. Uttering of death threats. Possession and distribution of a controlled substance. Meaning they weren't a real loss to our society."

"Why did they come here?" she asked, yet she already knew. Obviously, a hired killer coming after Hugo and she just happened to be in the wrong place at the wrong time.

"It is not unusual for criminals to flee here. They think we're easy, but we're not. We take crime seriously."

"I'm sure you do." She kept the sarcasm to herself.

"Curious, though, how they ended up on Mr. Laurentian's property."

"Most likely, they were going to rob him blind."

"Possibly. And you're sure you saw nothing?"

She shook her head. "Nap and then a shower. That's it." No body floating in the pool. That was only for her nightmares.

"And still no recollection of how you got that bump on your head?"

"Nope."

"You will call me if you do remember?"

"Of course," she lied.

Pierrot left, and she paced. One killer had been foiled, but Hugo remained in danger. Perhaps it was dumb of her to care, but there was something about the man that she couldn't let go. It bothered her how they'd left things between them.

The anger seething inside him.

She'd never meant to deceive him. But she wasn't sure he believed that. If only she had the nerve to speak to him again. Maybe find the right words...

What if she showed up at his gate, though, and he wouldn't talk to her? What if he hated her? What if... she actually acted instead of making assumptions?

She stared at the clothes hanging in the closet. So many beautiful things. Slinky, elegant, luxurious. The woman who wore those things didn't cower and let anything frighten her. This Meredith they'd told her about was a bold, take-charge kind of woman.

That woman wouldn't let something like a man's bad mood stop her from trying to make things right.

Before she could choose a dress of courage to wear, there was a knock at her door.

No real surprise. It had been a whole three hours since her last check-in. She swung open the door. "I'm fine. No, I don't remember anything yet, I—" The words trailed as she saw him standing there. "Hugo." Such pleasure infused her at the sight of him.

He shifted. "Um. You forgot this." He thrust the bathing suit at her.

He could have easily not bothered or had it couriered over. But he'd brought it himself. Surely that meant something.

"Want to come in?" She stepped aside and, for a second, nerves convinced her that he'd decline.

He crossed the threshold, and her heart hammered in her chest as she shut the door.

"Nice view," he said, looking out the window.

She snorted. "It's okay compared to the one from your place."

"Listen, I came to—"

"Hugo, I—"

They both paused as their statements clashed.

He inclined his head. "Go first."

"I wanted to say again how sorry I am. I don't know what real-me planned. But the amnesiac version of me never meant to hurt you or lie to you in any way."

"You didn't hurt me."

"Then you're the lucky one."

"Meaning what?"

A single shoulder lifted, and her chin ducked. "I thought after the night we spent—"

He interrupted. "That was sex. Nothing more."

"It felt like more."

"I'm not looking for a relationship. Never said I was."

Her nose wrinkled. "According to Carla, I'm the

same way. I like to keep it casual. Rarely going back for seconds."

"Keeping it emotion-free makes for fewer misunderstandings later on."

"With the only drawback being the years spent alone adding up." Her lips turned down. "I'm starting to wonder if I really want my old life back."

CHAPTER TWENTY-FOUR

"DID YOU JUST CALL ME OLD?" For some reason, he teased to lighten her mood. He couldn't have said why. He was still angry.

Her lips twitched a little. "Well, you do have more gray hair than I do."

"How would you know? You don't even know if yours is natural." He arched a brow.

"It's real. All of me is." She glanced down at herself, and his gaze followed. "No nips or tucks, apparently."

"Why mess with perfection." The unbidden words slipped from his lips.

But the smile she gave him was well worth the gaffe. "My passport says I'm thirty-four, you know. But, apparently, my real age is closer to forty-six." Her nose wrinkled. "I don't feel that old."

"Because you're *not* old. You're halfway there at this point. In your prime."

"Definitely didn't feel old last night." Her sultry expression had the desired effect.

He got hard. So fucking hard. Then muttered, "What am I going to do with you, Ariel?"

"You could do me." She moved into him, and he welcomed the feeling of her in his arms. "Turns out, I'm not seeing anyone."

"I don't know if that's a good idea." He said it, but his body argued it.

"Because of the age thing. I get it. Once a day is all you can manage. Pity." She shoved away from him, and he blinked.

The gauntlet had been thrown. His masculinity challenged.

"Oh, like fuck, Ariel." He reeled her back in, knowing she'd neatly trapped him and not caring.

He wanted to be inside her again. To see if that moment of connection had indeed existed, or if he'd imagined it. Perhaps it was a one-time thing.

He kissed her, but she only allowed a short embrace.

"Maybe you're right, and it's a bad idea."

"It's a terrible idea."

"The worst," she agreed, nipping his chin. "But..."

"We're both mature adults."

"Too mature."

"We really owe it to ourselves to have one last time. You know, on account of our advanced ages."

"To get it out of our system," she agreed.

"Then we're done," he murmured against her lips before he kissed her. A press of his mouth was all it took to ignite the passion. It simmered between them, hot and demanding. It didn't care that they were wrong for each other. When it came to lust and desire, they were perfectly matched.

Following a sensual rhythm, the mouths tasted. Caressed. Their breath a hot mesh of anticipation. Pushing her against the wall, Hugo dropped to his knees, her dress an easy thing to push up, baring her to him.

A touch of his fingers parted her thighs. It took only a small shove to have her drape it over his shoulder, truly exposing her to him. The pinkness of her beckoned, and he eagerly pressed his mouth to her. She shuddered and moaned, her excitement causing the core of her to pulse.

He felt it and had to take a lick.

Her hips bucked, meaning he had to grip her, hold her so he might keep licking and tasting. Lapping between her folds before flicking her clitoris. She jerked each time he jabbed it, and he wanted to feel her excitement. He thrust a pair of fingers into her, the heat and wetness gripping him as he continued to play with her clit. Teasing it. Tugging it. Her sex squeezed his digits. He pumped them as his tongue tickled her nub, flicking it as he thrust into her.

When she came, he felt it, tasted it. And he kept going. Taking that ebbing climax and rolling her into the beginnings of a second one. She panted and moaned, then squirmed free so she could kneel and shove at him, her hands going to his pants and tugging him loose. She gripped him, her fist tight, and she worked his cock, drawing a long, drawn-out moan from him.

"Lie down," she ordered. Forget all the perfectly fine beds and chairs and couches.

He lay down on the floor, and she positioned herself over him. Their gazes locked, and he held his breath as she lowered herself just enough to tease the tip of him.

He put his hands on her waist and pulled her down, sliding his thick shaft into her. Deep. Stretching. Filling her enough that her head fell back, and she moaned.

"Yes."

She rocked on him, slow, hard grinds of her body against his. He helped, his hands on her waist, helping to push him deeper. And when her breath hitched as he moved a certain way, he made sure to repeat that motion.

Over and over. Hitting her in that g-spot. Feeling her tighten. Knowing she was close to coming. Coming on his cock.

She dug her nails into his chest as she climaxed, the muscles of her sex squeezing him so tightly, he couldn't help but explode.

She collapsed atop him, his cock still inside her. Both of them breathing hard. His body and hers bathed in a thin sheen of sweat. He didn't want to move. Wanted to forget the outside world for a bit.

She said nothing.

What could they say? The chemistry between them didn't change the circumstances.

She'd lied.

He couldn't trust her.

She was a killer.

So was he.

It would end in someone being hurt—or dead.

But he still spooned her as he fell asleep.

CHAPTER TWENTY-FIVE

BEFORE DAWN, Merry snuck out of bed. Literally, squeezed out and tossed on a bathing suit before leaving the room. Not because she wanted to.

She wanted nothing more than to remain lying beside Hugo. The heavy weight of him, a soothing comfort.

Yet she had much to ponder. Such as what she would do since her memories remained stubbornly locked away. She also didn't know how to handle Hugo. They'd said one last time.

No promises.

No strings.

Problem was, she still desired him. Not love, though. Even she knew better than to think she could fall in love so quickly. But he was right, they couldn't be together. No matter how good it felt.

Exiting the building, the humid air and redolent

scents filled her senses. The resort was just starting to stir, sprinklers finished their cycle, leaving the foliage damp. The hint of the spray used to keep the bugs at bay, lingered in the air.

She began to walk towards the main restaurant where she could find coffee and a pastry. She could have called someone to bring it, and yet that would have meant spending more time with Hugo. He might have woken. Dressed. Left.

It might be cowardly, but she didn't want to deal with it.

As she followed the path she'd learned only the day before, mostly because her friends insisted, she noticed no one else up and about. A pity. There was something stunning about this time of day when everything was pristine and perfect.

The sound of an engine had her scooting to the side and glancing over her shoulder. A golf cart, the vehicle of choice on the resort, slowed and stopped. The man, younger than she, had a thick beard and mustache, sunglasses, and a hat pulled low, the logo for the resort stamped across both it and the shirt he wore.

"Give you a ride?" he asked.

"That would be lovely." She slid into the rear of the golf cart facing backwards. "It's a lovely morning."

"Umg." The driver grunted and pulled away, tires spinning and spitting gravel. She jolted and frowned as she grabbed a support bar.

"Careful."

No reply, nor did he slow down. The bright exteriors of the buildings flashed past with chunks of forest. He was taking a different route than she did on foot. They veered off the paved lane to a dirt one, the pitted surface jostling them hard enough that she got worried. "This isn't the right way." It suddenly occurred to her how stupid she had been, getting into a vehicle with a stranger. Had she forgotten those that'd tried to kill her?

She needed to get off. The moment the speed slacked a bit, she jumped, landing better than expected, her body going with the motion so that she hit with both feet, knees bent.

Pushing up, she began to run back down the path towards the resort and people. Safety.

Only the driver of the cart flipped around and came roaring at her. She veered for the woods, her breaths huffing as she ran wildly through the foliage, getting thoroughly lost, her panic making her pause as her chest heaved.

She had no idea where to go.

Not a sound other than those of the forest stirred the air. Birds cawing. The rustle of branches. The whine of insects.

A sudden prickling at her nape had her whirling. Too late to do anything.

The blow sent her into dreamland—with a hint of cloudy nightmares.

CHAPTER TWENTY-SIX

THE DOOR SLAMMED OPEN, and so did her eyes in response to the loud thud. The red, glowing digits on the clock showed that it was just past three a.m. The bar had closed and kicked everyone out. Tommy was home.

And Tommy didn't care if his antics woke her and the children.

She knew better than to say anything. Even the neighbors didn't dare complain, not anymore. Mr. Sandrowski still wouldn't meet her gaze if they passed in the hall.

Dealing with Tommy had that effect on people. He could be a mean man, especially when drunk. Even worse, she could see it coming. He'd have an evil light in his eyes. His lips would pull into an awful sneer. And the words that spilled from his mouth were designed to hurt as much as his fists.

She hated the nights he stayed until the bar closed because that meant he came home. Better when he spent his time elsewhere. She didn't care who he slept with. It saved her from him. A respite that would get her killed if she ever told him how she really felt.

Escape seemed utterly impossible.

Forget the cops. They couldn't help. Tommy knew it and taunted her with the knowledge.

"Call them," he said, eyeing her in a way she knew ended with her getting hurt. "Dial nine-one-one, and I promise I will slice myself,"—he held out the switchblade, waggling the shiny weapon—"and tell them you attacked me."

The cops might not believe him, but there might be enough doubt that they wouldn't put Tommy in jail. In the best-case scenario, they'd offer to put her in a shelter. It wouldn't keep her safe from Tommy.

When he said he wouldn't let her leave, he meant it. He'd kill her if she dared try.

She pretended to sleep despite the second slam of the door as he shut it. Tommy really didn't care about anyone else. Over time, she'd learned that bullies always did those things on purpose, hoping for just a tiny bit of defiance so they could justify their slaps.

At times, she wanted to hit him back. Punch him in the face and see how she liked it.

The satisfaction wouldn't be worth dying for, however, and one important thing stopped her. She couldn't leave her children motherless.

Tommy stomped into the bedroom, construction boots still on. He might be a raging, abusive drunk, but he did go to work. Hungover on Mondays, cleaning up enough during the week so he was just an asshole. Then payday arrived, and by Sunday, he was a hungover blob on the couch, moaning for her to be quiet.

She remained curled on her side, feigning sleep. She mustn't even twitch. She remembered to breathe shallowly. Let him think she slept hard. It wouldn't take him long to pass out once his head hit the pillow. He just needed to lie down.

Thump. Thump. Boots hit the floor. Then the *shush* of material followed. Tommy flung himself into bed, and her body rocked. It was hard to pretend to roll with it and fall into a natural, sleeping position.

Not for the first time, she wondered how it had gotten to this point. She blamed a dumb, young brain, and a shitty home life. A mother who didn't give a shit about her three kids with different dads. A stepdad who creeped her out.

She wanted to leave but didn't comprehend how. She'd met Tommy when she was too immature to know better. He wasn't as violent then. He'd pick her up from the house on his bike, and they'd ride, the wind in her hair—because only pussies wore helmets, at least according to Tommy.

When she got pregnant, he'd promised to love them both, forever and ever.

Those were the days that he'd fooled her. When a different Tommy promised her the world. The name-calling and slaps came later when, at age twenty-one, Tommy could legally get drunk. She should have left then. Instead, she'd had another kid. Hoped the old Tommy would come back.

He got worse, and now she was trapped. To survive, she had to play nice.

At least it was the end of the weekend, the cycle would reset for a few days. A bit of time where she might not want to sob.

The blankets were yanked from her so that Tommy might wrap himself.

She couldn't help but shiver.

He must have been watching because he verbally reacted. "Frigid fucking cunt."

Never the start to a good conversation. She tried to pretend sleep a while longer.

He shoved at her, hard enough that she yelped. No more faking. "Hey, Tommy. You're home." She could barely muster the fake sleepy enthusiasm he expected.

"Where else would I be? I pay for this dump."

Actually, she contributed too, but pointing that out was a guaranteed slap.

"I'm glad you're home."

"No, you're not, you frigid, lying bitch. And I've had it. I'm done living with you," he declared.

Could it be? Was he finally leaving? She held her breath.

"You and those brats are why I work so hard. Get up. Work. Go to bed. A guy never has time to have fun."

She could have pointed out the hours he spent on the couch watching television. Used to be they went for walks and out for ice cream. Rides on his bike and watching the sunset. "I'm sorry you have to work so hard." Never mind the fact that her days weren't any easier.

"You should be sorry. Look at what I come home to. A shitty dump and a cold cunt." His voice turned mean.

She'd be sporting bruises in the morning if she didn't do something right now. But he reeked of booze, sweat, and urine.

"I think we should both go to sleep and talk about it in the morning."

"You can't tell me what to do. I'll go to bed when I fucking please." He spat as he spoke, the spittle hitting her face because he just had to get close to her.

Why couldn't he just go to sleep? Permanently, would be nice.

"Go to sleep, Tommy. Or don't. That's up to you, but I have to get some rest because I need to get up with the kids in the morning."

"Those fucking brats. They don't even look like me."

Those so-called brats were his despite what he liked to think when drunk. Ages one and three. They tied her tighter to Tommy than she liked. She'd really wanted to leave after the first child, but he always found a way to drag her back in.

He threw out her birth control, and along came number two. She wished she'd had the gumption to run while her belly was still flat.

But he threatened to hunt them down and kill them if she did. As he said, *"If I can't have you, no one will."*

To prove a point, he sent her a picture the following day of him parked in front of the sitter's— Mrs. Alvarez, who minded her babies while she worked, in exchange for housework.

A shelter wouldn't save her from Tommy. He'd be a threat until the day one of them died.

The heavy stench of beer hit her in the face. Fetid and ripe. He grabbed her by the upper body, his thick fingers digging into her flesh. He leaned close, and everything about him stank.

"It's time you earned your keep."

"I pay for more than my fair share. More than you, sometimes." She couldn't help the bitter words.

Whack. The blow caused her to bite her lip. She glared at him.

"Want another one?" he snapped. "Now get on your knees and greet me like a proper girlfriend should."

"I am not blowing you. It is the middle of the night,

and I have to be up in less than two hours." Because the crack of dawn for some reason woke Donovan, no matter how she tried to black out the window in the other room. A two-bedroom for a steal because of the subway tracks running behind the building. On a warm day with the windows open, you could sometimes catch a breeze.

"You are such a fucking loser. In bed early. Always fucking tired. I'm tired, I work hard. But I still know how to have fun."

"Is that what you call getting drunk?"

"I drink because you're fucking boring. You do nothing."

"I have fun with the children."

"Leeches," he snapped. "Should have been the load you swallowed, maybe then you'd be fun again."

She almost replied, "*I grew up.*" But he wouldn't like that. She'd already pushed him too far. She needed to rein in her tongue and placate him.

"Why don't you get some sleep and, in the morning, I'll keep the kids quiet so you can rest. Then how about some nachos for the game?"

"Ain't nachos without beer."

"With beer," she promised. Which meant cutting a few things off the grocery list. She'd have to hit the food bank again. But the bribe worked.

Tommy rolled off her and heaved a soft sigh. Crisis averted.

Until the door opened, and Donovan, her baby boy

in superhero pajamas, stood there, moaning. "I don't feel good."

Tommy went off like a bomb.

"Get the fuck back to bed, you little whiner." The harsh rebuke hit their son.

Donovan began to sniffle, and a still very drunk Tommy hauled himself out of bed, wearing only his boxers.

He advanced on Donovan, who began to back away in fear. He didn't often see this side of Tommy. The daddy he knew, while abrupt, wasn't usually this drunk when the kids were awake. Donovan didn't budge when Tommy reached for him.

"Get the fuck to bed."

"Don't you dare touch him," she yelled. She didn't make it out of bed quickly enough before her son hit the floor hard, shoved by his father.

Tommy whirled, and his smile held a hint of wickedness as if he'd finally gotten what he wanted. "Are you going to tell me what I can do? I'm his father. I can do whatever I like."

Between one heartbeat and the next, he was on her, hand on her throat, bending her back, making her gasp with the fear and pain of it.

Donovan didn't like it at all. He ran for Tommy and pounded on him with tiny fists.

"No hurt my mommy."

Tommy kicked his leg and sent his son flying. The little body flew. Like literally lifted off the floor, and then hit. Her baby slammed against the wall hard and then fell to the worn parquet floor. Donovan didn't move.

She froze. Blinked as Tommy continued choking her.

Had he just killed her baby? Her sweet Donovan?

My.

Baby.

The strength came from out of nowhere. A place she'd never been able to touch before. A well of rage and grief swamped her. She broke out of Tommy's hold and ducked under his arm when he would have grabbed her again. She ran for Donovan and scooped him up as she bolted for the other room, a living room with a small kitchenette attached.

In her arms, Donovan's breath hitched. He was alive but petrified with fear. Hurting, too. Because of Tommy.

He'd almost killed her baby.

That's it. I'm done. It was one thing to hurt her, but not the children. Never the children.

Rather than flee, she set Donovan down in the kitchen. She couldn't leave, not without Caroline.

Tommy stomped out of the bedroom, his once-flat belly already starting to pooch. His rictus of anger shone clearly in the light from the subway line that came through the dirty window.

He'd torn down the blind a month ago, and she'd not been able to afford to replace it.

"I'm going to call the cops," she stated.

"With what phone?" he sneered.

She actually had a reply for that. She reached into the box of healthy cereal he'd never touch and pulled out a prepaid cellphone she'd bought on a clearance rack and kept charged for emergencies—such as this. "With this one."

"Proof you've been plotting to have me taken to jail. You want to take my kids from me. Ungrateful bitch. After all I've done for you."

Donovan whimpered at her feet and drew Tommy's hard glare.

"You should have been nicer to me." He didn't head for her but the other bedroom, the one with the baby.

She didn't think at that point. Next thing she recalled, she hung from his back like one of those monkeys seen in documentaries. But those sweet creatures weren't stabbing anyone.

She had her fingers around the hilt of the kitchen knife sticking out of Tommy's flesh. He staggered inches from the crib he'd salvaged during one of his *nice* days.

She slid from his back, knife in hand, panting as he turned and gaped at her. In his eyes, she saw the one thing she'd craved for a while now.

Fear.

About time he knew how it felt.

"Help me. Call. Nine-one-one." His breathing

hitched and blood bubbled at his lips. He reached out pleading hands to her. She took a step back. She wasn't about to get too close.

She stood and watched until he stopped moving, then called the emergency line. Once she hung up, she grabbed the baby, who'd somehow remained asleep. She sat in the living room with Donovan snuggled close when the cops arrived, kicking open the door.

The jolt of memory as they rushed in screaming, "Don't move or we'll shoot," roused her from a deep sleep. The disorientation proved extreme as her past as Anita, the battered girlfriend, vied with the present, which involved a throbbing head.

Great. Another lump. What would she forget this time? Her sweet babies, solemn-eyed Donovan, and dimply cheeked Caroline? Maybe the fact that she hadn't been Anita in a long time.

Hold on.

She blinked as she realized, *I know my name.* Knew her current name, and all the past ones. Could see Donovan and Caroline in her mind's eye.

She remembered everything. The despair as she sat in the jail cell, not at the thought of spending her life behind bars, but upset because she would lose her babies. At the time, she'd consoled herself with the fact that at least Tommy couldn't hurt them anymore.

And then she ended up getting a second chance. Recruited by Marie. Brought into the Killer Mom fold, where she excelled at her job. It was more wonderful than she could have imagined. Flying to fancy destinations, seducing the occasional billionaire, and discovering a sense of purpose and pride that made her days with Tommy seem like a distant nightmare.

But the one thing she never did get over was her fear of commitment. Oh, she'd gotten married. A few times, as a matter of fact, almost all a result of deep undercover operations. Meredith, the name she'd chosen upon her rebirth, didn't have the same hang-ups about sex that other women did.

For one, she never attached any emotion to it. Not anymore. Sex was like exercise. Grunt a little. Sweat a little. If the guy wasn't incompetent, maybe even climax. When it came time to walk away, she did so without looking back.

In the case of some of her husbands, she killed them when she was done using them. Accidents were an excellent way to cover up the mission's completion. An unfortunate mishap where he slipped and cracked his head before falling into the pool and drowning. Another had a heart attack behind the wheel. The third had been murdered by his mistress, who was double-crossing him.

Meredith had lived a full life, and her children had gotten nothing but the best, never knowing she led the life she did. She'd made enough that she could retire, especially given that her children had finished prep school and gone on to university, both graduating with honors and landing decent jobs.

But then what would she do? Stay at home and bake all day? She still felt young and energetic. She might live another thirty or forty years. She wasn't ready to retire.

The throb in her head lessened, and she rolled to her back, noticing that she was untethered and lying on a bed in a small room with a round window. A cabin on a boat. A nice one, but not exactly superb. She'd travelled on much nicer vessels.

As to how she'd gotten here... She moved from the past into the now. She recalled leaving Hugo, the naked sprawl of his limbs a temptation. What was it about the man that made her lady parts melt?

Had he been the one to knock her out? No, because she recalled hitching a ride on her way to breakfast from a resort employee. At least she'd thought he worked there. And then, stupid Ariel—not Meredith because she would have known how to spot a fake cab driver—was attacked. Meredith wanted to groan at her naivety. The good news...she'd gotten her memories back, which meant she wasn't helpless anymore.

Rising, she noticed that she still wore the same summer dress she had on before, if creased from lying on it. Standing on feet that had lost the sandals she wore, she felt the slight rocking of the boat.

Glancing out the porthole, she couldn't see much, couldn't even tell the time of day. She might have been out for hours or minutes. The good news was that whoever had kidnapped her evidently wanted her alive.

The door opened at her touch, and she found herself in a richly appointed room that might have been nicer without the gun pointed at her.

"About time you woke up."

"I'm sorry, do we know each other?" she asked, facing the driver of the golf cart. He still had the thick beard and mustache, but he'd ditched the resort uniform for khakis and a button-up shirt, the fasteners open halfway down his chest.

"We never had a chance to meet because you killed my father and took what should have been mine."

CHAPTER TWENTY-SEVEN

HUGO WOKE ALONE in the bed with the hideous flowered coverlet. No red hair on the pillow beside him. No morning cuddle or sex. Meredith had left.

Probably for the best. So, why did it burn? Usually, he was the one sneaking off, leaving Gerome to get rid of overnight guests. He hated the awkwardness that came when he had to douse their expectations. In that moment, he understood how humiliating it could feel.

He dressed, cursing his stupidity and weakness in hunting her down the day before. She had to have seen through the lame excuse he'd used in returning her swimsuit because he couldn't just show up and say "*hi.*" Couldn't admit that he wasn't ready to say goodbye.

Still wasn't. Their last time had been even better if possible. Her body a perfect fit to his. But good sex wasn't enough. He needed trust, too.

Despite taking more time to get dressed than his simple garments warranted, she didn't return, and he felt pathetic stalling. Hugo returned home and spent a few hours pretending to work, but in actuality, he wondered what Meredith did. Did she think of him at all? Remember the pleasure of their bodies coming together, their rhythm impeccable?

Would she perhaps be the one to hunt *him* down? Was it wrong to hope that she would?

And what of the fact that he'd slept? Soundly. Deeply. Past the witching hour and right until dawn. The second time with her. Not something that ever happened with anyone else.

He didn't recall any nightmares. Didn't suddenly wake, his eyes wide and staring, hearing his sister's voice on the phone. The pleading. The gunshot.

The guilt.

It didn't assuage it one bit that she'd drawn him into that life. She'd married a gang leader. As her brother, he was drawn into that world, and when the abuse began, he took his sister out of it.

Unfortunately, it didn't end well. Killing Agneaux didn't bring back his sister or his nephews.

Almost two decades later, and he still dwelled on it.

Wondered what things in Meredith's life had made her into a spy and probably a killer.

He sighed as his mind went back to her. He left the room, pathetically hoping he'd see her. Maybe she'd gone to get them coffee or breakfast. Perhaps she was an early morning jogger.

He made it to his car without seeing anyone but staff. Got home after stopping to eat. The food was bland, and his mind was definitely elsewhere.

Gerome greeted him at the door, but Hugo could only grunt when asked, "How was your night?"

The night was good. The morning could have used a do-over.

And then it got worse.

The agents of KM barged into his office with Carla leading the way. The group of them were dressed to kick some athletic ass. Yoga shorts and capris, snug tanks, hair in ponytails with thunderous expressions.

"Where is she?" Carla bellowed.

"Excuse me?" Hugo looked away from his laptop, not startled at all given he'd seen their arrival on the cameras. "Where is whom?"

"Don't play dumb. Meredith. Ariel. Whatever you want to call her. She's missing."

His brows pulled together. "Well, she's not here."

"Says you."

"Yes, says me."

Carla huffed.

"You spent the night with her." Stated by the blonde. She tapped her phone. "Hotel surveillance footage shows you entering her room yesterday and not leaving until this morning."

"It shows me leaving alone."

"Because you hired someone to do your dirty work," Louisa accused.

"Are you all insane? We slept together. Nothing more. If she's missing this morning, then maybe it's because she had an appointment."

"She would have told us," Audrey interjected.

"Damned straight, she would have. We know she was kidnapped."

"Not by me," he stated.

"If you don't have her, then you won't mind if Louisa and Audrey take a peek around," Carla challenged.

"Knock yourselves out." He waved a hand, and off the women went. "She's not here, though. And I don't know why you automatically assumed I kidnapped her."

"We know you had an accomplice. We saw her with him."

"Are you talking about Gerome? Because I am pretty sure I can vouch for the fact that he didn't. How long has she been gone?"

"No one has seen her since the crack of dawn."

The words made his blood run cold. It was late morning now. "Maybe she's at the spa?"

That got him a snort. "Just because we're women, doesn't mean we spend our days getting pampered."

"Just because she's missing, don't assume that the last man she slept with did it," he snapped right back.

"Did you have her killed?" Carla accused.

"For what? Now you're being ridiculous." Hugo started drumming his fingers on his desk. "I would never kill her."

Left unsaid was: "*as long as she didn't deserve it.*" Hugo wasn't one to let a little thing like death stop him from doing what was necessary.

"Am I being ridiculous? You were pretty pissed when you found out who she was. Maybe you wanted revenge." Carla leaned low and hissed the words.

"My idea of revenge is bankrupting people and then buying their prized possessions for nothing." He'd started doing it after he realized just how much his crimes hurt the innocent. The death of his sister turned him into a hunter. He went after the bad people and used their ill-gotten gains to do good. To his surprise, it proved more profitable than a life of crime.

"Ugh, now you sound like Tanya. Why kill them when you can drain their 401Ks and flag them at the IRS for life?" Carla's voice pitched to mimic her friend.

"You say that now, but who did you call when they tried to audit you because you decided to claim ammo on your form?" Tanya huffed.

"I wasn't lying. I needed those bullets for work." Carla shrugged.

"Can we get back to Meredith? What makes you think she's missing? Maybe she just wanted some time alone. Has anyone checked the hospitals?"

"Already done. She hasn't been seen since she hitched a ride on that golf cart with that guy."

"What guy?" he asked. "If he was the last one to see her, then why aren't you questioning him?"

"We tried. Only we can't find him because he's not an employee. Obviously, some kind of hired thug," Carla mused aloud with an accusatory glare in his direction.

"For fuck's sake, he doesn't work for me." Hugo snorted. "In case you hadn't noticed, Gerome is my man when it comes to special jobs."

A knock at the door had them looking to see Marie stepping inside. "Ladies. I thought we weren't going to bother Mr. Laurentian anymore."

"Merry's missing. We think he did something." Carla jabbed a finger in Hugo's direction.

"For the last fucking time, no, I didn't." His patience eroded.

"He's telling the truth." Marie held up her phone. "Which you would know if you'd investigated instead of going off half-cocked."

"What did you find?" Tanya asked.

"Proof it wasn't him. Time to leave, ladies."

"I'll go find Louisa and Audrey to let them know," Tanya said, leaving the office.

"What kind of proof?" Hugo asked.

"Nothing you need to worry about. Sorry to have bothered you." Marie went to take her leave, but he stood and barked, "*Sorry* won't cut it. I am involved, and I want to know what's going on. Where is Ariel? I mean, Meredith."

"I don't know where she is at the moment, but according to the latest report, she was last spotted being dumped into the trunk of a car about a mile from the resort."

"What? We have to find her," he exclaimed.

"Meredith is our top agent. If anyone can escape and look good doing it, it's her," Carla stated, showing she paid attention despite watching something on her phone.

"Except she doesn't remember that she's an agent!" he snapped, realizing in that moment the truth: she truly had lost her memory.

"We are aware and will handle it. This isn't your problem anymore," Marie stated.

"I am making it my problem," he growled.

"Why? You've made it clear you think she's a liar and couldn't wait to give her the bum rush." Carla once more didn't give him any quarter.

The KM operative glared at him, and he resisted the urge to fidget.

"Why does it matter what I think? Once you find her, it's not like we're going to see each other again." A thought he didn't actually like.

"You're right, you're not, because you're obviously not good enough for her," Audrey said with a sniff as she returned with the others.

"We should have let her marry him and then iced his ass," Louisa replied. "Can you imagine getting this place to vacation?"

"It would make a nice honeymoon spot," Carla mused. "Question is, do we kill him before or after the ceremony? Philip might notice."

"We are not killing Hugo," Tanya declared. "Even if he is a jerk where Merry is concerned."

"And to think, this jerk was going to offer the use of his toys if you needed them in a rescue."

"What kind of toys are we talking about?" asked Audrey.

"Fast and expensive ones."

There was a collective *oohing*.

"No more fast toys for you," Marie said with a shake of her finger at Audrey.

"Ha. You got told," Carla crowed.

"Is now the time to tell Mother you were puking this morning."

That brought an excuse. "I ate something that was off."

"You're pregnant," Audrey declared.

"We don't know that for sure yet."

"Until we do, I think you should be grounded from going fast, too," Marie said with a pointed frown at both women.

"Thanks a lot, tattletale," Carla muttered.

Before things devolved further, Hugo interceded. "Does Meredith have a tracking device?"

"We don't chip our agents," Marie retorted hotly.

"It might be an idea, though," Tanya mused aloud.

Hugo paced behind his desk. "Since the person

who took her did so under false pretenses, it will be more difficult to track him."

"We're running his image through our databases to see if we get a hit," Tanya remarked.

"Should run it through Laurentian's personnel file, too," Louisa suggested.

"Go right ahead. I've nothing to hide. I'm more concerned that we might not succeed, or it will take too long. There must be a better way to figure out who took her before they kill her."

"Why would they kill her?" Marie sounded surprised by the very idea. "She's no use as a hostage if she's dead."

"Hostage for what?" Hugo couldn't help but sound genuinely confused.

"In exchange for you."

He blinked. "Me? What makes you think this is about me?"

"Why else take Merry?"

"Because she works for you. Maybe this is a KM shakedown."

"Seems more likely the perp knows you're lovers."

Lovers. Hardly. They'd fucked. Epically. But more than that...he wasn't ready for anything more, was he? Then why did it bother so much that she was gone? "Are you sure it's about me and not her? What about the attacks? The attempts on her life?"

Blank expressions met him. "What attacks? She never said anything to us," Marie said slowly.

He quickly told them of all the incidents, and by the end of it, Carla was pacing and cursing. "Fuck, this changes everything. If someone targeted her directly, then this is personal."

"Think someone from a former mission recognized her?" mused Audrey aloud.

"Could be. Or someone ordered a hit because she foiled some plot. There was that thing with the Russians a few months ago."

Russians? Missions? The Ariel he thought he knew grew more complex by the minute. And if he was truthful, more intriguing, too.

"We need something more concrete than possibilities," he growled.

"If this is vengeance, could be they'll take her off the island given we've never worked here before. I'll check the airlines," Audrey declared, moving away with her phone.

"I'm going to see what surveillance systems in the city and other resorts I can hack into to run facial recognition software on their feeds," Tanya offered.

The others began cross-referencing the island with names gathered during former missions.

Whereas he pulled up the file compiled by the Killer Moms on him. He read it front to back.

Nothing jumped out. "This has nothing in it. I want to see your file on Ariel."

"Why?" Marie asked.

"Because maybe there's something in there that an

outsider will spot. After all, if the person is on this island, I'm more likely to recognize them than you."

"Her basic info won't help you," Marie said.

"I'm not asking for the basics. Give it all to me."

Marie's lips pressed into a tight line. "She won't like it. There are very personal things in her file. Events no one should know about."

"You really think I'm going to talk?" He arched a brow.

"If you do, then I think you understand the consequences." Marie tapped the screen of her phone. "I'm air-dropping it to you now. Keep in mind the file cannot be shared or copied."

"And will self-destruct when I'm done. I get it," was his reply as it landed on his screen.

He read it and found himself more fascinated than expected. The woman born as Anita Whittaker did not have an easy life. Born in poverty, a victim of violence at home, then later on, domestic abuse. It could have ended badly for her, especially once she killed the bastard who'd hit her.

Hugo never could abide a man who hit a woman.

Anita turned a difficult life around. Kind of like him. They had more in common than he would have believed.

It was by accident that he stumbled upon the clue.

"She was married to Hector Gonzalez?" Hugo asked suddenly.

"A few years ago, why?" Marie immediately replied.

"Because just before Hector died, I acquired most of his business assets."

"Hostile takeover?" Tanya asked.

"Very. And the son wasn't happy. Claimed I'd stolen his inheritance."

"Wait, I remember this. Wasn't the kid in jail?" Carla exclaimed aloud.

It took Tanya but a moment to dig up the information. "Hector Gonzalez Jr. was incarcerated for fraud when his father died. He contested the will the moment he was sprung, but it went nowhere. Merry inherited it all."

"Meaning Hector has reason to hate both Ariel and me." A motive to hurt them.

In moments, there was silence and furious key clicks as they sought information on Hector Jr.

They began to shout out their findings, "One Hector Gonzalez Jr. moved to the Bahamas about six months ago."

"According to financials, Hector Jr. has a few toys and a cool eleven mill sitting in the bank."

"And he's single," Audrey announced.

"Holy shit, you won't believe this but—"

"Hector is the one who put out the hit on me," Hugo said, interrupting Carla. "Meaning, he probably was the one going after Meredith, too. The question is, where is he?"

It didn't take long to pull a list of places Hector had been seen. A rental condo in the city, and a yacht. A quick phone call to the marina revealed that the boat had left its slip earlier that day.

Find the vessel, and they'd probably find Meredith. Hopefully, alive. He took it as a good sign that she had been taken rather than just shot.

"Which of my toys should we take to find him? Helicopter or speedboat?" he asked.

It turned out they wanted both.

They just didn't want him along.

"Thanks for your help, but we've got it from here," Carla stated.

"I should—"

"What?" Carla asked, standing toe-to-toe with him. "It's not like you've got a personal stake when it comes to Merry."

"Now, Carla, we don't know his intentions," Tanya said, kind of siding with him.

"No intentions. I just want to make sure she's safe."

"We'll send you a text," she announced, the wind of the rotor blades tugging the strands of her hair. Louisa and her girlfriend Rosy had already taken off in the boat. Tanya sat at the controls of the chopper. Portia, as co-pilot, gestured to Carla, who got permission to go if she promised not to get into an actual fight. Audrey and Marie would form a mobile command post.

They took off to save Meredith without him. Hugo

EVE LANGLAIS

could have walked back into his office and gotten
drunk. What did he care? Whatever happened next
was out of his control. They'd either find her or they
wouldn't. Not his problem. They were equipped to
handle hostage situations.

But he couldn't stop thinking about her. How she'd
called him her hero. He'd saved her how many times?
What if she needed him to save her again?

His phone chimed. A text message from an
unknown number. It had an address he recognized and
a simple message. *I have your girlfriend. Be here by six,
or she dies.*

In that moment, he realized how much her safety
and wellbeing mattered to him. "Motherfucking
bastard!" he yelled. Seething, the art on his wall
narrowly avoided getting tossed to the floor and
stomped. He needed to vent. To act. But rushing
wouldn't help either of them.

Think.

Hector obviously wanted him to walk blindly into
a trap. The idiot chose the wrong man to mess with.

Emerging from the house, he found Gerome
waiting by the Porsche. He handed Hugo his holster,
then a jacket to cover it. He took one look at Hugo's
face and declared, "I'm driving."

Rather than argue, Hugo said, "Take us to the old
sugar factory."

Because, apparently, Hector had decided to have
his little showdown at the company property that used

to be family-owned for generations until Hugo took it at auction after forcing it into foreclosure.

The sun beat down mercilessly as they drove. He'd already sent message to KM and wondered who would get there first. The helicopter ran into turbulence and had to land. The boat started its search in the opposite direction.

It was up to him

The luxury car slowed to a creep past the rusted gates. He'd already dropped Gerome a quarter-mile away. Let Hector Jr. think he'd come alone.

Slowing even further, Hugo eyed the construction zone comprised of skids of wood, a large waste bin, and a dingy trailer they kept locked at all times. Hector and family might have neglected the company that made their family famous, but Hugo planned to restore the old factory with some modern improvements. Once it opened, it would create jobs and real money, not the fake stuff previously laundered.

The lagoon flowing past the factory held a ship bobbing at a dock.

The urge to pull his gun hit Hugo the moment he left his car. But he didn't want to seem too threatening. He cautiously approached. For all he knew, Hector Jr. had a scope trained on him and would shoot.

He counted on the fact that the guy would want to vent or gloat. Why else send him a text? If he wanted him dead, then a sniper could have done the job.

The ship appeared eerily silent, bobbing gently.

No one on deck. Nor any voice to greet him—which made the sudden rocking and thumping startling. There was a yell. More banging.

What happened? Grabbing the ladder bolted to the side, he climbed aboard the ship, swinging himself onto the deck, a quick glance at the wheelhouse showing it empty. The stairs going down were narrow and put him at a disadvantage. Gun in hand, he tripped down and emerged into a lounge with a body on the floor. Across the room from it, Ariel sitting on a table, looking rumpled but uninjured.

Her smile upon seeing him proved bright and happy. "Hugo!"

"Thank fuck you're all right." He dragged her to him and kissed her thoroughly.

The embrace was a hot and passionate thing. In between pants, she said, "I remember who I am."

"That's good," was his reply as he slid her some more tongue.

"I remember everything about you, too." She reached down to cup him.

He had the sense to say, "Later. I should check—"

"He's dead." She cupped his cheeks, her gaze intent on him. "I killed him."

He could see that she expected him to react. "Thanks for saving me the trouble."

She said nothing for a moment. "I guess this is a good time to say I've read—and now remember—your report. I know what you do. I read about your sister and her family."

So much for thinking she saw only the public persona. "How? The file Marie showed me had nothing in it."

"I have my sources. And I don't always share them. Especially when it's private stuff."

He leaned his forehead on hers. Guess I should confess that I saw yours, too. Anita."

"Anita is dead. She was a weak and stupid girl."

"She was a brave woman and mother."

"My babies are everything to me," she said softly.

"And you kept them safe." Unlike him with his family.

As if reading his mind, she cupped his cheeks. "We can't change the past. We can only do better for the future."

"Is there a future?" he murmured.

"I'm more of a *now* person. As in, right now, before we're interrupted." She tugged at his pants.

He thought about turning her down. They couldn't be together. They were so different, and yet the same in their brokenness. She was alive. And perfect.

She unbuttoned his pants as he slid her skirt up over her legs. The table was the ideal height for fucking. The tip of his cock passed over her sex and found her wet and ready. He thrust into her, his mouth hot and panting against hers as her fingers dug into his shoulders.

The climax proved fast and furious.

And when it was done, he held her in his arms.

"One last time?" she whispered against his lips.

What if he said he would never have enough? "Maybe that was hasty."

"Very hasty. After all, we're both adults who can surely handle a few more rounds to truly sate this strange desire between us."

"Why strange?"

She didn't answer, nor would she meet his gaze. She gave him a slight push, and he pulled away.

"Why is it strange?" he prodded, and yet he understood. Because after all the times he'd been betrayed, he suddenly found himself ready to try again. With her.

"Because I'm not supposed to have a hard time walking away." Her lips turned down. "Why did you have to be so damned sexy and charming?"

His lips tugged up at the corners. "What happened to arrogant?"

"Part of your appeal. I like a man with swagger."

"And I like a woman with confidence." He stroked a few strands of hair from her cheek. "My beautiful and feisty Ariel."

"It's Meredith, actually."

"I know what your name is, but to me, you'll always be my redheaded mermaid." He rolled a shoulder.

"I can't believe you named me after a cartoon," she

huffed and then laughed. "Guess I know what I'm going to be for Halloween this year."

A good thing he'd tucked his dick away, or she'd have seen how much he liked that idea. Now, he just had to find a way to be around when it happened.

But first things first. She hopped off the table and went across the space to the body. A single shot to the head.

"I see you know how to shoot."

She smiled. "Sugar, I know over a hundred ways to kill a man."

"Call me sugar again, and I am going to put your ass back on that table for another fucking."

"Promise?" She winked. "But hold onto that thought for later. We've got a wedding to attend. Look at the time."

She pushed past him and went out onto the deck. He followed.

"What about after the wedding?"

"What do you mean?" she asked, shading her gaze as the afternoon sun hit a bright pitch.

Would she really make him say it? "How long are you staying on the island?"

Her gaze strayed to his for a second. "Does it matter?"

He should have said that it did. Admitted that he didn't want her to go. Not yet. That he'd like to get to know her better.

But that was when the helicopter appeared, and

she clapped her hands. "Oh, now that's a nice toy. Yours, I assume?"

"It is."

"Thanks for letting the ladies borrow it. See you at the wedding."

He still didn't say anything.

When the helicopter landed, blades whipping hair and loose debris, she ran for it and hopped inside. Not even a wave goodbye.

What did he expect? They'd said no strings. No commitment. And yet...there was something between them. He would swear she felt it, too.

As the helicopter lifted, he hopped off the yacht and headed for his car, noticing Gerome leaning against it. Smoking.

"Since when do you fill your lungs with that shit?" he asked.

"Says the hypocrite with a penchant for cigars."

"That's completely different," Hugo defended. Cigars were to be savored, and not too often to truly enjoy them.

"I take it Junior won't be a problem anymore?" Gerome eyed the boat.

"Ariel took care of him."

"Then we should get going if you're going to make the wedding on time."

"Who has a sunset wedding?" he grumbled even as he had to admit, they were rather spectacular.

"It's romantic," Gerome rumbled as he grabbed the

bottle with the rag sticking out of it. He lit it and tossed it onto the boat.

Boom. Flames danced along the wooden deck. Out of control. Kind of like Hugo's passion for Ariel.

Would he feed that fire by taking a chance, or let it fizzle?

He discovered the answer at the wedding.

INTERLUDE: THE WEDDING

CARLA APPEARED A BIT GREEN, Marie noted, looking around for the nearest bucket.

"I'm going to puke," Carla stated, leaning forward to hide between her legs, her filmy, white gown frothing around her. Her hair was loose for once and had flowers weaved in it.

"You are not going to puke," Tanya reassured.

"Not to mention, it's called morning sickness for a reason," Audrey baited.

"Puke on that dress and Merry will kill you." Portia's reminder.

"A wedding. What was I thinking? We should have lived in sin." Carla eyed them balefully. "Who convinced me to do this?"

"You want to do this," Tanya soothed. "You love Philip."

"I do, but what if it doesn't work?" Carla practically hyperventilated.

"If it doesn't, then I'll make sure no one can trace the lye I have to order to get rid of the body. No trails will lead back to us," Portia offered.

"You guys are the best!" Carla's lips wobbled, and Marie stepped in.

"Hush now, my sweet girl. You deserve this. All of this. The perfect wedding on the beach. A person to love you and be a father to Nico." Marie meant every word even as she knew her best agent would never return to work for her. Another of her foundlings had fled the nest.

"But—But—" Carla's lip wobbled. "What if everything changes?"

"It will. For the better." The ladies moved in for a hug, and mascara threatened to run.

"Oh, hell no! Everyone stop what you're doing!" Meredith boomed. "Don't you dare make the bride cry just as she's about to walk down the aisle. Game faces on. Places, people," she snapped. "It's go-time!"

There had been a few suggestions on ways to shake things up for the wedding. Jump from a plane and parachute in. Parasailing onto the beach. A palanquin carried by nubile bearers. Even a boat racing onto the shore, and the couple leaping from it.

In the end, Carla wanted something traditional, and Merry made sure she got it while Marie took care of the expenses.

The hotel rolled out a red carpet. Literally. The white fold-up chairs had frothy red and white bows. The groom wore a tux, even in this heat. All of his groomsmen did too, their arms linked with their respective bridesmaids for the walk up the aisle. The bridesmaids proved quite elegant in their slate-gray dresses, their bare legs catching the breeze.

Tanya looked especially radiant while a certain Bad Boy agent by her side appeared nervous. Marie had seen the ring. Devon had nothing to worry about.

When the music shifted, and it was time for Carla to appear, Audrey started to sob—later blaming her pregnancy hormones.

Marie bit her lip lest she sob too, because of all the people Carla could have chosen to walk her down the aisle, she'd chosen Marie. Because as Carla said, "It's because of you that I'm getting a chance at this life, this happiness."

Her happily ever after.

As Marie looked around at her girls. Each of them handpicked, each a precious daughter and sister and best friend, she could only hope they would all find someone who would look at them how Philip looked at Carla.

CHAPTER TWENTY-NINE

LOOKING AWAY PROVED IMPOSSIBLE. Meredith snuck more peeks at Hugo than she should have. After the boat, she'd not known what to think. He'd come to her rescue. But he'd made no promises. No plans.

Was it over? Did she want to see him again? The answer surprised.

And then he'd sent her a note. A *note* of all things, written by hand, therefore personal, and yet just ink on paper.

For the most intriguing treasure to ever come from the sea. We should talk.

Accompanied by the most delicate set of pearl earrings with a matching necklace. What did it mean? Why the gift? And talk about what?

Because she didn't want to talk. Seeing him in the

crowd, looking incredibly delicious in his cream-colored suit, she wanted to strip him and...

His gaze met hers and locked on. She might have stared at him forever if not nudged. "Merry, it's over."

Her cheeks flushed with heat, and she ducked her head. She could only hope the twilight covered any color.

The boisterous crowd moved to the beach and the tent set up on it. If anyone thought it strange to see killers barefoot in the sand, dancing, eating, and talking like ordinary people, then they'd better keep their mouths shut, or Meredith would take care of them.

Nothing would mar this special day. When the mothers were brought into the Killer Mom agency, they were often broken and frightened things. Timid. Flinching. Powerless. Afraid.

And then they were shown how to take that power back. To fight and face the world with their heads held high. They discovered that they could be successful and happy.

But at the core of everyone, man or woman, they wanted many of the same things. Acceptance. Companionship. And the most elusive thing of all, true love.

At her age, Merry knew whatever chance she had for a normal relationship had long since fled, and she should know better than to feel that flutter of hope when she looked at Hugo. How many times had it been crushed?

What if this time, she made the right choice?

"Why so serious?"

The depth of his voice never failed to bring a shiver. She turned and, rather than give Hugo the coy answer that would start the flirting game, chose the bold truth.

"Ever wonder if you'll be alone forever?"

"That is a serious question for a wedding." He glanced around at the smiling faces before meeting her gaze once more. "The answer is yes. After so many betrayals, it's hard not to feel jaded. To wonder what the angle is every time a smile is directed your way."

"I've been used."

"We both have."

"I have a hard time forming attachments."

"Which sounds like me, except I'm having a hard time detaching from a certain mermaid who washed up on my beach."

She could have accepted the branch he extended, but she wasn't about to go into this with any secrets. "I've killed all of my former husbands."

"Does this mean I'm safe so long as we don't get married?"

Her lips curved. "Why, Mr. Laurentian, are you asking me to go steady?"

"I'm asking you to see where this thing goes."

"What if it goes sideways?"

"What if it doesn't?" He shrugged. "I'm thinking it's time I took a chance."

Before she could reply, she heard Jacques calling to her.

"Mademoiselle, I hear you have your memories back."

Meredith whirled to see him in full uniform. He'd better not ruin Carla's reception.

She pasted on a bright smile. "Superintendent, so nice of you to check on me at my friend's wedding."

"More than check, I'm afraid. We need to have a talk, seeing as how upon our investigation of the death of Hector Gonzalez Jr. and senior, we happened upon a photograph in his apartment." Jacques whipped it out of his pocket.

Hugo swiped it from his hand and, without even looking, held it to a tiki torch.

The police chief's mouth widened. His eyes did, too.

Marie took that moment to slide her arm through his. "If it isn't the very attractive chief of police. I was just telling someone about how well you do with such limited resources. It just so happens they've been looking for a new charity they can donate to, and what better cause than public safety?"

Marie led the inspector away, and Meredith smiled coyly at Hugo. "Care to dance?"

"I don't know if I can hold you close without wanting to strip you."

She licked her lips. "We can't leave yet."

"How long?" His impatient desire for her only enflamed her. "A few hours."

"Hours?" He groaned.

"Don't worry, sugar. My flight doesn't leave for another two days."

"You need to cancel that flight."

"Oh, I do, do I?" She arched a brow. "I can't suddenly forget I have a life and home just because you want us to have a fling."

"Good point. Is this your way of asking me to go with you?"

"Would you?"

"I'm sure I can manage some time at your place."

She blinked. "Are we actually talking about dating?"

"Dating is so eighties." He laughed.

"I happen to love that decade." She flipped her hair. "But I don't miss the hair. Do you know how much work went into getting the bangs fluffed that high?"

"How did we get to bangs from going steady?"

"I don't know if I'm ready for steady."

"Oh, for fuck's sake, kiss already," Gerome grumbled, stomping past.

There were literally fireworks as their lips locked.

And she did end up canceling her flight.

EPILOGUE

THE AGENT KNOWN as Cougar Mom, the one feared by the newest batch of KM recruits, shoved her sunglasses higher on her nose. She was nervous. So very, very full of anxiety, and Hugo knew it.

He held her hand tightly. "It will be okay."

"What if it's not? I've never had my babies meet a man before."

Hugo shook his head. "I still don't know how that's possible. You were married numerous times!"

"I never brought my work home," she mumbled. It was always, "*Mommy is going away for a few weeks on business.*" She'd never dated anyone worthy enough to meet her babies.

"Are you sure I look okay?" he asked, finally showing signs of nerves as people began to trickle out of the airport's arrival area.

"Good enough to strip and eat. Pity we don't have time to find an empty closet somewhere."

"That was just mean, Ariel."

"I know. Which reminds me, if the kids ask, that's just your nickname for me." Her new identity would take time for her kids to learn about. But she was ready to leave old Meredith behind. Ariel was a woman in love who didn't fear commitment. Just ask the giant engagement ring on her finger.

He'd done it without warning, merely dropping to one knee. No speech. Just two heartfelt words. "Marry me."

She'd said *"yes"* before she even saw the ridiculously beautiful ring.

Her babies emerged side by side, tall and dark-haired Donovan, still so serious after all these years, and his ginger-haired sister, Caroline.

She needn't have worried about their reaction to meeting Hugo because the first thing her son said upon holding out his hand for a shake was, "About time, Mom."

Caroline muttered, "Think if she gets laid, she'll lighten up and stop bringing over containers full of treats whenever she's not out of town on business?"

Her cheeks heated. "I do not bake that often."

"I haven't seen you bake lately at all," Hugo said, his grin more than wicked. His fault she didn't have the time. Between her recruiting and training of new agents

—most which would flunk out or move on before hitting the field—and sex...on the beach, in the hot tub, in bed, the car, and every other place they could think of—she barely had time for virtual brunch with her friends.

But that was a good thing. Happiness kept her busy.

As the kids walked ahead of them to the car, she leaned close to Hugo and whispered, "I'm not wearing panties."

To which both her babies exclaimed, "Ew, Mom. Gross."

Because, apparently, moms didn't have sex.

Later that night, after Hugo had finished kissing every inch of her, they snuggled, and he said, "I got a weird present today from your friend Carla."

"What kind of gift?" she asked, sprawled across his chest.

"A t-shirt that says *I <3 MILFs*. What the hell is a milf?"

Meredith laughed as she whispered the answer in his ear then gasped as he made her come again because it turned out moms *could* have sex. And love. Even at her age.

BACK IN THE USA...

Picking the twins up from school, Portia noticed something. All the kids milling in the yard and on the sidewalks were doing something: bouncing a ball, chatting with friends, shoving each other, or chasing. Not her girls.

They stood side by side, alone, looking uncannily tidy alongside their peers. At their young age, they shouldn't be so serious.

When was the last time she'd seen them play? What about exercise? Was she parenting them wrong? She'd read all the books. So many of them. Her daughters were brilliant, and already way ahead of their peers scholastically.

But she had obviously forgotten what it was like to be the smart kid in school. The way other kids shunned her. It wasn't too late, though.

On the drive home, she saw the solution to getting them out of the house and not only meeting new kids but also learning a skill, which was how she camouflaged the idea.

"You want us to learn to kickbox?" Mae said with a wrinkle of her nose.

"I don't want anyone to hit me," Lin added, just as repugned.

"This is about learning how to protect yourself," Portia encouraged. "It will be fun."

The girls proved less than enthused until they met their instructor, Ted.

POOR TED NEVER IMAGINED THE TROUBLE HE'D

GET INTO WHEN HE DECIDED TO HELP THE PRETTY SINGLE MOTHER. BUT HE'S READY FOR THE CHALLENGE—IF A TIGER MOM WILL GIVE HIM A CHANCE.

LOOKING FOR MORE EVE LANGLAIS ROMANTIC SUSPENSE?

CHECK OUT BAD BOY INC.